'... ...
post-war existential fiction. By any standards: a masterpiece'
The Independent

'While the book is no longer topical, it has lost none of its appeal as a tale of survival against the heaviest of odds'
Daily Mail

'*Rogue Male* is probably the most famous chase thriller ever, influencing an entire generation from Frederick Forsyth to Lee Child'
Catholic Herald

'This is a completely terrific read, a perfect example of its kind and one we'd recommend to lovers of classic thrillers'
Eastern Daily Press

'We are in classic British adventure thriller territory – think Buchan – with an upper-class Englishman showing his stiff upper lip to best effect . . . A page-turner if ever there was one!'
Good Book Guide

Born in Bristol in 1900 and educated at Magdalen College, Oxford, Geoffrey Household worked all over the world, including Eastern Europe, the USA, the Middle East and South America, as, among other things, a banker, a salesman and an encyclopedia writer. He served in British intelligence in the Second World War. His other works include *A Rough Shoot*, *Watcher in the Shadows*, *Rogue Justice* and an autobiography, *Against the Wind*. He died in 1988.

By Geoffrey Household

The Spanish Cave
The Third Hour
The Salvation of Pisco Gabar
 and Other Stories
Rogue Male
Arabesque
The High Place
A Rough Shoot
A Time to Kill
Tales of Adventurers
Fellow Passenger
The Exploits of Xenophon
Against the Wind
The Brides of Solomon and
 Other Stories
Watcher in the Shadows
Thing to Love
Olura
Sabres on the Sand
The Courtesy of Death

Prisoner of the Indies
Dance of the Dwarfs
Doom's Caravan
The Three Sentinels
The Lives and Times of
 Bernardo Brown
Red Anger
The Cats to Come
Escape into Daylight
Hostage – London
The Last Two Weeks of
 Georges Rivac
The Europe That Was
The Sending
Capricorn and Cancer
Summon the Bright Water
Rogue Justice
Arrows of Desire
The Days of Your Fathers
Face to the Sun

GEOFFREY HOUSEHOLD

ROGUE MALE

An Orion paperback

First published in Great Britain in 1939
by Chatto & Windus
This new paperback edition published in 2014
by Orion Books,
an imprint of The Orion Publishing Group Ltd,
Orion House, 5 Upper St Martin's Lane,
London WC2H 9EA

An Hachette UK company

7 9 10 8

Copyright © Geoffrey Household 1939 and 2014

A CIP catalogue record for this book
is available from the British Library.

ISBN 978-1-4091-5583-6

Typeset at The Spartan Press Ltd, Lymington, Hants

Printed and bound in Great Britain by Clays Ltd, St Ives plc

The Orion Publishing Group's policy is to use papers
that are natural, renewable and recyclable products and
made from wood grown in sustainable forests. The logging
and manufacturing processes are expected to conform to
the environmental regulations of the country of origin.

www.orionbooks.co.uk

To Ben
who knows what it feels like

One evening in the spring of 2005, my friend Roger Deakin telephoned to relate a mystery and propose an adventure. Into his postbox the previous day had dropped an envelope containing a handwritten letter, a marked-up section of the 1:25000 Ordnance Survey map for south Dorset, and a photocopy of several pages from Geoffrey Household's classic 1939 thriller, *Rogue Male*. The letter explained that the map showed the likely location of a deep lane in which Household's nameless hero – pursued across Europe by Nazi assassins – eventually goes to ground, and where the novel reaches its extraordinary climax.

The photocopied pages included Household's detailed description of that lane. It was a 'deep sandstone cutting' that ran over 'the ridge of a half-moon of low, rabbit-cropped hills, the horns of which rested upon the sea, enclosing between them a small, lush valley.' The cutting was 'a cart's width across' at its bottom, and above its high banks rose hedges from which 'young oaks leap[ed] up'. Its floor was choked with 'dead wood' and jungled by 'nettles . . . as high as a man's shoulder', and its entrances and exits were barred by 'sentinel thorns'. 'Nobody but an adventurous child would want to explore it', noted Household.

Roger was sixty, but his nature was that of 'an adventurous child', and he was excited. For him – as for me, as for so many post-war English schoolboys – *Rogue Male* had been a formative book, that had buried itself in his imagination at an early age. The idea of exploring the landscape in which it took place was irresistible to him. He suggested that we travel to Dorset and locate the holloway hideout. We would sleep in the open at night, and try to keep to cover as we moved, in gentle emulation of our fugitive hero (though unpursued by Nazi assassins).

So it was that a few months later we drove down to Dorset together, and set off on foot, on a hot July morning, from near the little village of North Chideock. We had map, novel and letter in hand, our rucksacks were packed with billhooks, billycans and sleeping bags, the sea was hazing blue to our south and the half-moon ridge of hills was sloping green to our north. It felt like a fine and boyish escapade – a happy regression. We should, of course, have guessed that it would not be as simple a matter as we thought to track down our hero's bolt-hole. We should have known that this cult book about concealment, escape and evasion would not give up its secrets so easily.

Geoffrey Household was as old as his century. Born in 1900, he was too young to fight in the First World War, though the shadow of that conflict fell upon his later life and writing. He was schooled in Dorset and Bristol, graduated in 1922 with a first-class English degree from Oxford, and spent most of the rest of the '20s working in Romania, France and Spain – first as a low-grade banker and then as a banana salesman. But what he wanted to be was an author, and to this end he resigned from the banana company in 1929 and moved to Hollywood and then New York, scraping by as a short-storyist for magazines and a screenwriter for the Columbia Broadcast System. By 1933 he was back in England, poor and unemployed, spending days walking the Wiltshire and Dorset countryside while working out his next move. It came in the form of another sales job, this time for an ink manufacturer, which required of him the itinerant existence that he relished: trips through the Scandinavian and Baltic countries, Mediterranean Europe and South America. As he travelled he wrote, and literary success ensued at last in the form of a novel commissioned by *The Atlantic Monthly*, which was published as *The Third Hour* in 1938.

In December of the same year, Household began work on *Rogue Male*. He wrote it fast, in a matter of months. It was serialized in the summer of 1939 and then published in book form shortly afterwards, just as Europe tilted into war. The novel is, unmistakably, his masterpiece. It re-defined the genre of which it was part. It became an instant bestseller. It was quickly issued in a Services and Forces special edition by Chatto & Windus, as buck-up reading for British troops in the early months of conflict. It was filmed – poorly – by Fritz Lang as *Man Hunt*, which premiered in America in 1941 and was acclaimed by interventionists as another prompt to join the European war. Ian Fleming's James Bond series, David Morrell's *First Blood* (in which the character of Rambo first appears) and Frederick Forsyth's *Day of the Jackal* all bear the clear marks of its influence. It has been several times adapted for television and radio, and the dark-green cover of its 1950s Penguin edition, re-printed onto t-shirts and coffee mugs, has become a lifestyle accessory and post-ironic man-gift. I am still awaiting sight of the camp parody – *Rouge Male* – that has surely, somewhere, been written.

So renowned is the novel, in fact, that during Household's lifetime it proved hard for him to evade its presence, either in terms of the critical reception his numerous later books would receive, or in terms of his own literary imagination. The plots and themes of the later novels often repeat with variation those of *Rogue Male*: fugitive heroes, subterranean hideaways, and a chthonic relationship with the life-giving land. In a curiously reflexive manner, Household found himself unable to escape the symbolic space he had carved out in his best book.

Household more than once described himself as 'a sort of bastard by Stevenson out of Conrad', and at first glance the literary genealogy for *Rogue Male* appears clear enough. Robert Louis Stevenson's *Kidnapped* (1886) – in which Alan Breck and Davey Balfour are chased across the Scottish Highlands by English redcoats in the 1750s – began the 'hunted-man' genre. John Buchan's *The Thirty-Nine Steps* (1915) – in which Richard Hannay is chased across the Scottish Lowlands by German agents – updated it for an age of geo-politics and aerial warfare. And Graham Greene's *A Gun For Sale* (1936) – in which a hired killer called Raven is chased from Central Europe to the British Midlands – extended its geographies and reversed the logic of pursuit, such that the assassin became the quarry. From these writers, unmistakably, Household learned the skill of pacing and the propulsive narrative power of the hunt.

From Joseph Conrad, I think, Household learned how to pattern a novel intricately without slowing down its story, and he also learned restraint: in particular, the technique of omitting explicit description of key events. In Conrad's *Lord Jim*, only the awful consequences of the *Patna*'s impact with a floating spar are told – never the impact itself. In *Rogue Male* vital incidents go similarly un-detailed: the torture scene, the death in the Aldwych tunnel, the narrator's first visit to the holloway with his fiancée. Only the outcomes (wounds and scars, guilt, repressed trauma) of these episodes are alluded to; they are experienced chiefly as their after-maths. It is no coincidence that the narrator's eye is brutally damaged early on, leaving dancing patches of shadow where light should be; or that the novel should, over its course, draw tighter and tighter, down to a cave in the side of a lane whose shadowy interior seems 'fifty feet of solid blackness'. For so much of *Rogue Male* concerns things – actions, perceptions, memories – that occur out of sight or in darkness. Camouflage and cover are the novel's preoccupations; enigma, disguise and indirection its styles of telling. Even the narrator remains nameless throughout, only an 'I' – as artful at concealing his identity and character from his readers as from his pursuers. Artful too (it turns out) at concealing himself from himself.

I first read *Rogue Male* twenty years ago, fast and un-reflectively, pulled onwards by the need to know what happened next. It was only later, and on several re-readings, that the complexities of its patterns began to reveal them-selves to me. For this is a novel of elaborate and profound design. There are paired concepts – 'cover' and 'open', 'surface' and depth' – that repeat and weave. There are images and figures – notably the sunken track, the tunnel, the cave or den, and skins and skinning – that recur dozens of times in different forms. There are tiny details of incident or comment that anticipate or recall earlier versions of themselves. And there is the sustained analogy between land and mind, whereby the narrator's access to his buried emotions is enabled only by means of a literal digging down into the Jurassic bedrock of southern Dorset.

'It's curious how much cover there is on the chalk downs', Household notes casually at one point, 'prehistoric pits and trenches, tree-grown tumps, gorse and the upper edge of coverts, lonely barns and thickets of thorn.' His novel, likewise, appears to possess an uncomplicated surface – but is in fact riddled with hidden features. It is far more than just a thriller, and more too than a parable of moral pragmatism, individual self-reliance and an English brand of survivalism.

It is a novel, in fact, that requires of its readers a hunter's instinct. To discover its deep strangeness, you need cautiously to cut for sign, to track marks in its landscape, and to watch for disturbances to the expected.

If you've never read *Rogue Male*, stop right now and do so. There are serious spoilers ahead – and besides, who would want to be reading this introduction when you could be reading the novel for the first time?

Back? Good. It probably only took you a few hours. You'll now know the tumult of its opening few pages. So much happens, fast and disorientingly. Slowly, we piece together a plot. Our anonymous narrator, armed with a 'Bond Street rifle', illicitly enters a European country (that resembles Germany) and over several days stalks a dictator (who resembles Hitler) to his country residence. Using skills honed as a big-game hunter, he gets within sniping distance of his quarry. There is an opportunity to fire, but at the vital moment he is over-powered by a sentry. He is detained, interrogated, tortured, and put over a cliff in the hope that his murder will be taken as an accident when his corpse is found. But he falls into a marsh whose softness saves his life. He crawls from the marsh, desperately wounded, takes refuge in a larch tree by a river, evades the first search sweep, and then begins – painfully and it seems hopelessly – to make his way downstream towards the coast. His torturers come after him: the hunter is now the hunted.

The narrator's suffering in these first pages is appalling, but he recounts it with an eerie calmness. Understatement is his specialism: a mode of speech that combines self-protection, self-delusion and modesty. 'I had been knocked about very considerably', he observes. Indeed: during the interrogation he has had his fingers crushed, his fingernails pulled out ('Shirt buttons were quite impossible'), and his left eye has been smashed at with a tool of some kind, then burnt. His subsequent fall from the cliff has also ripped large areas of skin and flesh from 'the back of my thighs and rump'. 'I had parted,' as he sanguinely puts it, 'obviously and irrevocably, with a lot of my living matter'.

This fleshly maceration, this gouging out and stripping away of human 'matter', is the symbolic preparation for the conversion he will undergo in the novel's course. Before he can rebuild himself, he must be transformed. It is tempting to follow the lead of the title, and suggest that he changes into a hunted animal, wounded and dangerous – a rogue male. Certainly, he does identify himself in creaturely terms: he is 'a wounded crocodile, all slime and blood', a 'damned snake', a 'resting mammal'. But the conversion is more plural than this, for as well as becoming part-animal he also becomes part-earth, part-rock and part-tree – a hybrid version of the landscape itself. The marsh that saves his life in the cliff-fall coats him as healing poultice and a second skin. He at first imagines its 'blood-tasting mud' to be an 'extension of his body', part of the 'pulped substance' of his flesh. He is 'a creature of mud, bandaged and hidden in mud'; if he moves too fast, patches of his new mud-skin fall off and he bleeds from the gap. Once he has emerged from the marsh, he climbs into a 'prolific' larch tree whose boughs support him and whose needles conceal him. Wedged there, briefly safe, he feels as if he is 'growing to' the tree. When he at last descends, he picks up two branches as crutches and shuffles forward on them: he has become larch-limbed.

So begins the escape of this mud-tree-beast-man from the country of his sort-of crime. That escape is excruciating, patient, audacious and unlikely. He is helped along the river by a local man who lends him a pair of 'loose leather gloves' to hide the damage to his fingers (another of the skins he sheds and gains). The river leads him to the sea, and at the sea he wins the trust of fine Mr Vaner, the lusty first mate on an English merchant vessel. Vaner allows him to stow away in an empty water tank (the second of his several dens), which after the days of pursuit is comforting in the cover it offers: 'I had gone to ground after the hunt, and the cold iron of the closed tank was more protective than the softest grass in the open.' Once back on English soil, however, he realizes to his dismay that the hunt is not over. He is still prey, and has to continue his flight from danger and his search for refuge. 'I must bury myself', he decides, 'until the search for me had slackened'. After a fight with an enemy in the Underground (a different kind of sunken track), he decides to flee to Dorset: 'a remote county', as he unexpect-edly describes it – a landscape of 'green depths'.

It is into Dorset – deep England – that the novel then descends for its brilliant second half. He crosses the county by means of its old ways – 'narrow tracks', footpaths of long usage, 'a remnant of old Roman road' – covering his traces as he goes, and laying false trails in the hope of throwing off the sinister Major Quive-Smith, his chief pursuer. At last he locates the holloway to which he realizes he has been unconsciously heading since leaving London. Concealed in its shadowy and thorn-barred depths, he digs out a small cave in the lane's side, its 'roof and walls of earth and its floor of sandstone'. This is his den, his fox's 'earth', his hare's 'form', his 'safe pit of blackness'. His only companion is a local tomcat, who he nicknames Asmodeus. It is out of this womb-tomb that he will eventually be reborn.

On the hot morning that Roger and I set off in pursuit of *Rogue Male*, the path we followed up into the 'half-moon of hills' was clearly the beginnings of an ancient sunken lane, cut down ten feet or more into the orange sandstone of the area. We were excited – had we discovered the holloway already? Soon the lane deepened, and thickened with shoulder-high nettles. Blackthorn and hawthorn grew out into it, blocking easy passage; there were big coiled strongholds of bramble; and above our heads the trees that hedged the lane – oak, holly, ash, sycamore – meshed with one another to form an interlocking canopy, turning lane into tunnel. Surely this was the place? We pushed our way onwards, whacking at the nettles with sticks and slashing back the thorns where necessary with the billhooks. I cut my hand on a briar, and bled proudly onto the map.

Near the summit of the western horn of hills, the path became so overgrown that we had to leave it. We scrambled up its steep eastern sandstone side, and into the bright air of the flower meadow that bordered it. A few hundred yards further along, in a gap in the hedge by a towering ash tree, we found a way back down and abseiled into the holloway's depth, using ivy as our rappel-rope. We kept walking up, and occasionally came to little clearings where light fell and grass grew. Any noise we made thudded into the banks, and was lost. A person might hide out undetected in such a place for weeks or months, I thought.

Here and there we stopped to consult the novel, trying to map Household's descriptions onto the actual landscape. It took us a couple of hours to realise what we should have anticipated from the start: that Household had laid a false trail. Certain details corresponded perfectly. The 'ridge of a half-moon of low rabbit-cropped hills', with its 'outer or northern slopes' looking down upon the Marshwood Vale, was unmistakably the ridge that curled around Chideock and North Chideock. And the holloway we had found so quickly was bordered by 'an acre of pasture', its hedges were 'grown together across the top', and it was marked here and there by dead oaks, each of which was 'a paradise of wood-pigeons'.

In other respects, however, the book frustratingly refused to match the real world. Household's holloway ran northwards and 'downhill into the Marshwood Vale', but ours ran uphill on the south slope of the ridge. Our holloway was stone-sided and high-hedged on one side only; on the other, it fell away through a screen of holly to silage fields. There were two farms visible from our holloway, but their positions did not coincide with the positions of the farms of 'Pat' and 'Patachon' in the novel. We spent the rest of the day trying to locate our hero's refuge – and failed. Nothing would quite fit. Discrepancies persisted. Only late on did we realise that this was wholly in keeping with the novel. Household had smartly disguised his book's geographical secret, even as he appeared to give it away. We had been thrown off the scent – and that was itself a kind of teaching. He had even warned us plainly in advance, though we had failed to heed him: 'It is not marked on the map', he had written of the holloway.

Our exploration helped us to make sense of *Rogue Male* in other ways. Again and again, we encountered versions in the actual landscape of the novel's tropes of concealment, pursuit and excavation. Countless creatures had burrowed into the soft sandstone to make their dens – mason bees, rabbits, badgers. Buzzards turned and wheeled above us like spotter-planes. A woman dressed in red appeared on the curve of a hill, looked down upon us, then disappeared as if carrying the news of our presence to another. Once, a roe deer picked its way nervously into the middle of a field, until something unseen startled it and it escaped in urgent, arched bounds. And down in the valley we found a tiny Catholic chapel, dedicated to the memory of the 'Chideock Martyrs' — recusants who had illegally worshipped their faith in the hedges and copses of the area in the late sixteenth and early seventeenth centuries, at risk to their lives. These men and women had been tracked and chased through the country-side by the enforcers of Protestantism. Eight were caught: seven were put gruesomely to death, and one had died in prison.

At the end of the day, as dusk was settling, Roger and I returned to our original holloway hide-out, dropping down by the old ash tree into the darkness. We cleared nettles and briars, moved loose trunks to make seats, and then Roger built a fire — a tiny pyramid of small sticks with a hot centre of tinder, that produced an intense and almost smokeless fire. Sitting around the flames, we read out passages from *Rogue Male* and discussed the day's discoveries. That night, we slept in bivvy-bags in the meadow, preferring the expanse of the pasture to the dark confines of the lane. I remember that it was a clear and star-filled sky, and that I thought of our hero's cry as he lay trapped and helpless in his sandstone burrow: 'By God, I want to die in the open!'

The section of the novel in which Major Quive-Smith interrogates the narrator in his den is magnificent and unexpected. For several days, the Major tries sophistically to coax a signed confession out of his prisoner. The episode might be understood as an early study of Stockholm Syndrome, as a Catholic confessional in which the den's ventilation shaft serves as the grille, or as an extended psychoanalytical session. While the narrator despises Quive-Smith, he also respects him both as tracker and cross-examiner. And it is Quive-Smith's questions that at last permit the narrator to discover and confront the 'grief' he experienced at the murder of his fiancée by German state security, and the 'hatred' that he felt for those who had killed her. In analytical terms, he is finally able to face up to the trauma of her death, and to understand his cathexis of grief into lethal intent. In Catholic terms he is able at last to confess the pre-crime of his intended murder. None of these revelations is, paradoxically, possible until he has been concealed in his subterranean penitentiary, and until Quive-Smith's interrogation has 'destroyed all possible self-deception'.

The narrator's psychological interior is the novel's last hidden terrain, and its access completes the book's ongoing processes of digging and rupture ('I had gone beyond worrying about the state of surfaces', the narrator observes in the opening pages, after his body has been shockingly delved into by his torturers). In terms of character, we are now far from the gamesome resilience of Sapper's Bulldog Drummond or Buchan's Richard Hannay. Household's hero is a hunted and haunted man, unsure of his allegiances and unsteadied by modernity (it is notable that the 'bright aluminium' of the home-engineered sidecar betrays his presence to his pursuers, while the traditional nickel of the whisky flask deflects a bullet and saves his life). 'You are symbolic of the English', Quive-Smith tells him, in one of the many clunky lines in the screenplay of *Man Hunt*. Perhaps – but if so then the 'English' of 1939 are a dark and complicated people, not the stiff-upper-lipped and smilingly shallow Anglo-Saxons of cultural cliché. 'I distrust patriotism; the reasonable man can find little in these days that is worth dying for', writes the narrator. 'But dying against – there's enough iniquity in Europe to carry the most urbane or decadent into battle'.

The novel's brilliant climax involves his unlikely break-out from the den. Like some proto-Macgyver, the narrator realizes that the means of his liberation are the everyday objects lying around him in his prison – including the corpse of Asmodeus, who has been shot by the Major and then stuffed into the den to fester. It is Asmodeus who provides the final goad and inspiration. His body is ingeniously weaponised; cat is converted to catapult. The last of the novel's many tunnels is drilled into the cranium of Quive-Smith by an iron spit, fired from an improvised ballista of feline rawhide, bricks and ash-wood. The last of the novel's many skinnings occurs when the narrator assumes Quive-Smith's identity, and escapes England using the Major's documents as his own. And the last of the novel's many burials comes when, safe at last in Morocco, he drops Quive-Smith's passport into a hole in the ground in a sun-dried hill valley above Tangier. 'My escape was over', he reflects, 'my purpose decided; my conscience limpid.' He falls to sleep in the valley, his 'face in the short grass by the water's edge', his 'body drawing strength from that warm and ancient earth', preparing himself to go to war.

Geoffrey Household's own war was not wholly unlike that of his hero. Eighteen months after the publication of *Rogue Male*, he was appointed to Field Security, the department charged with military and civil security, and with espionage and counter-espionage: or, as he put it in his autobiography, with 'the defence of the army against the enemy agent'. He led a unit in Greece as the country fell in spring 1941, he impersonated a German spy in the Levant, and he acted as negotiator between De Gaulle's Free French and the Vichy government troops. While in Jerusalem, he met a Hungarian woman called Ilona Zsodos-Gutman, whom he subsequently married, and with whom he shared his post-war life. They lived together in southern England (Dorset, Devon,

Buckinghamshire and Oxfordshire), and had three children. Household's post-war career was a comfortable one, and though none of his other novels would ever enjoy quite such acclaim, he lived safe in the knowledge that in *Rogue Male* he had written a straight-up, stone-cold classic.

After Household's death in October 1988, his son decided to scatter his ashes in the *Rogue Male* holloway. When he went looking for the lane, however, in the half-moon of high ground above the Marshwood Vale, he found it impossible to establish its precise location. In the end he chose a spot in the open air, near the top of a hill that overlooked the whole landscape.

– Robert Macfarlane

Acknowledgements

Thanks, for various kinds of help, to Roger Deakin, Stanley Donwood, Geoffrey Household, Leo Mellor, James Purdon and Daniel Richards.

'The behaviour of a rogue may fairly be described as individual, separation from its fellows appearing to increase both cunning and ferocity. These solitary beasts, exasperated by chronic pain or widowerhood, are occasionally found among all the larger carnivores and graminivores, and are generally male, though, in the case of hippopotami, the wanton viciousness of old cows is not to be disregarded.'

cannot blame them. After all, one doesn't need a telescopic sight to shoot boar and bear; so that when they came on me watching the terrace at a range of five hundred and fifty yards, it was natural enough that they should jump to conclusions. And they behaved, I think, with discretion. I am not an obvious anarchist or fanatic, and I don't look as if I took any interest in politics; I might perhaps have sat for an agricultural constituency in the south of England, but that hardly counts as politics. I carried a British passport, and if I had been caught walking up to the House instead of watching it I should probably have been asked to lunch. It was a difficult problem for angry men to solve in an afternoon.

They must have wondered whether I had been employed on, as it were, an official mission; but I think they turned that suspicion down. No government – least of all ours – encourages assassination. Or was I a free-lance? That must have seemed very unlikely; anyone can see that I am not the type of avenging angel. Was I, then, innocent of any criminal intent, and exactly what I claimed to be – a sportsman who couldn't resist the temptation to stalk the impossible?

After two or three hours of their questions I could see I had them shaken. They didn't believe me, though they were beginning to understand that a bored and wealthy Englishman who had hunted all commoner game might well find a perverse pleasure in hunting the biggest game on earth. But even if my explanation were true and the hunt were purely formal, it made no difference. I couldn't be allowed to live.

By that time I had, of course, been knocked about very considerably. My nails are growing back but my left eye is still pretty useless. I wasn't a case you could turn loose with apologies. They would probably have given me a picturesque funeral, with huntsmen firing volleys and sounding horns, with all the big-wigs present in fancy dress, and put up a stone obelisk to the memory of a brother sportsman. They do those things well.

As it was, they bungled the job. They took me to the edge of a cliff and put me over, all but my hands. That was cunning. Scrabbling at the rough rock would have accounted – near enough – for the state of my fingers when I was found. I did hang on, of course; for how long I don't know. I cannot see why I wasn't glad to die, seeing that I hadn't a hope of living and the quicker the end the less the suffering. But I was not glad. One always hopes – if a clinging to life can be called hope. I am not too civilized to be influenced by that force which makes a rabbit run when a stoat is after him. The rabbit doesn't hope for anything, I take it. His mind has no conception of the future. But he runs. And so I hung on till I dropped.

I was doubtful whether I had died or not. I have always believed that consciousness remains after physical death (though I have no opinion on how long it lasts), so I thought I was probably dead. I had been such a hell of a time falling; it didn't seem reasonable that I could be alive. And there had been a terrifying instant of pain. I felt as if the back of my thighs and rump had been shorn off, pulled off, scraped off – off, however done. I had parted, obviously and irrevocably, with a lot of my living matter.

My second thought was a longing for death, for it was revolting to imagine myself still alive and of the consistency of mud. There was a pulped substance all around me, in the midst of which I carried on my absurd consciousness. I had supposed that this bog was me; it tasted of blood. Then it occurred to me that this soft extension of my body might really be bog; that anything into which I fell would taste of blood.

I had crashed into a patch of marsh; small, but deep. Now, I think that I am alive — today, that is, for I still hesitate to describe myself as alive with any permanency — because I couldn't see or feel how much damage had been dealt. It was dark, and I was quite numb. I hauled myself out by the tussocks of grass, a creature of mud, bandaged and hidden in mud. A slope of scree rose sharply from the marsh. I had evidently grazed it in my fall. I didn't feel the pain any longer. I could persuade myself that I was no more seriously hurt than when they put me over the cliff; so I determined to move off before they came to find my body.

I had, though I didn't then know it, a good deal of time to play with; they hadn't any intention of finding my body until it was stiff and there were independent witnesses with them. The unfortunate brother sportsman would be accidentally discovered with his corpse undisturbed, and the whole history of his fate perfectly plain on the nasty sloping rock from which he had slipped.

The country at the foot of the cliff was open woodland. I remember nothing except that there were thin shadows and thick shadows. The image in my mind is so vague that they might have been coverts or clouds or waves of the sea. I walked about a mile, I suppose, and chose a thick darkness to faint in. I came to a sort of consciousness several times during the night, but let it slide away. I wasn't returning to this difficult world till dawn.

When it was light, I tried to stand on my feet, but of course I couldn't. I made no second effort. Any movement of the muscles interfered with my nice cake of mud. Whenever a crust fell off I started to bleed. No, I certainly wasn't interfering with the mud.

I knew where there was water. I had never seen that stream, and my certainty of its direction may have been due to a subconscious memory of the map. But I knew where water was, and I made for it. I travelled on my belly, using my elbows for legs and leaving a track behind me like that of a wounded crocodile, all slime and blood. I wasn't going into the stream – I wouldn't have washed off that mud for anything in the world; for all I knew, my bowels were only held in by mud – but I was going to the edge.

This was the reasoning of a hunted beast; or rather, it was not reasoning at all. I don't know whether a sedentary townsman's mind would have worked the same way. I think it would, if he had been badly enough hurt. You must be badly hurt to reach the stage of extinction where you stop thinking what you ought to do, and merely do it.

I made the trail look as if I had taken to the stream. I crawled to the edge and drank, and turned myself round in a shallow, a safe two inches deep, where the signs of my wallowing would be washed out. They could track me to the cover where I had lain up for the night, and from there to the water. Where I had gone when I left the water they would have to guess.

Myself I had no doubt where I was going, and the decision must be credited to my useful ancestors. A deer would trot upstream or downstream and leave the water at some point that the hunter's nose or eyes could determine. A monkey would do nothing of the sort; he would confuse his tracks and vanish into a third dimension.

When I had turned round in the shallows, I wriggled back again – back and back along the damned snake's track I had made. It was easy to follow; indeed it looked as definite as a country lane, for my face was only six inches above the ground. Thinking about it now, I wonder that they didn't notice, when they followed me to the stream, that some of the grass was bent the wrong way and that I must have gone back on my tracks. But who the devil would think of that? There aren't any laws on what print a man leaves when he's dragging his belly – and on such a monster of a trail there was no apparent need to look for details.

The outward journey had taken me under a stand of larch, where the earth was soft and free of undergrowth. I had brushed past the trunk of one tree which I now meant to climb. The lowest branch was within two feet of the ground; above that were another and another, sweet-smelling sooty branches as close together as the rungs of a ladder. The muscles of my hands were intact; I had gone beyond worrying about the state of surfaces.

Until I was well above the level of a man's eyes, I did not dare rest boots on branch; they would have left caked prints that no one could miss, I went up the first ten feet in a single burst, knowing that the longer I held on to a branch the less strength remained to reach the next. That half-minute was just a compelling of one hand above the other: two pistons shooting alternately from heaven knows what cylinder of force. My friends have sometimes accused me of taking pride in the maceration of my flesh. They are right. But I did not know that I could persuade myself to such agony as that climb.

The rest was easier, for now I could let my feet bear my weight and pause as long as I wished before each hoist. My legs were not limp; they were immovable. That was no disadvantage. I couldn't fall, wedged in as I was between the little branches of that prolific tree. When I climbed into the narrowing of the cone and the boughs were thicker and smaller and greener, I got jammed. That suited me well enough, so I fainted again. It was luxury, almost sin.

When I became conscious, the tree was swaying in the light wind and smelling of peace. I felt deliciously secure, for I was not looking forward at all; I felt as if I were a parasite on the tree, grown to it. I was not in pain, not hungry, not thirsty, and I was safe. There was nothing in each passing moment of the present that could hurt me. I was dealing exclusively with the present. If I had looked forward I should have known despair, but for a hunted, resting mammal it is no more possible to experience despair than hope.

It must have been the early afternoon when I heard the search-party. As they worked down the slope to the north of my tree I could watch them. The sun was in their eyes, and there was no risk of them spotting my face among the soft green feathers of the larch which I pushed aside. So far as I could tell, my legs were not bleeding; drops falling on the lower branches would be the only immediate sign of my presence. The slight bloodstains from my hands were there to be seen if anyone looked for them, but, on black boughs in the half-lit centre of a tree, not readily to be seen.

Three uniformed police were trampling down the hillside: heavy, stolid fellows enjoying the sunshine and good-humouredly following a plain-clothes man who was ranging about on my trail like a dog they had taken for a walk. I recognized him. He was the House detective who had conducted the first part of my examination. He had proposed a really obscene method of dragging the truth out of me, and had actually started it when his colleagues protested. They had no objection to his technique, but they had the sense to see that it might be necessary for my corpse to be found and that it must not be found unreasonably mutilated.

When they came nearer I could hear scraps of their conversation. The policemen were looking for me with decent anxiety. They knew nothing of the truth, and were in doubt whether I had been man or woman, and whether the case had been accident or attempted suicide. They had been notified, I gathered, that a cry or a fall was heard in the night; then, unobtrusively guided by the detective, they had found my knapsack and the disturbance in the patch of marsh. Of course I could not work out the situation at the time. I could only receive impressions. I was growing to my tree and aware of immense good nature as I listened to them. Later on, I made sense of their words.

Seeing my reptilian trail disappear into the stand of larch, the House detective perked up and took command. He seemed certain that I should be found under the trees. He shouted to his three companions to run round to the other side in case I should escape, and himself crawled under the low boughs. He nearly gave the show away there, for I was supposed to be eagerly awaiting help; but he wanted to find me himself and alone. If I were alive, it was necessary to finish me off discreetly.

He passed rapidly beneath my tree, and on into the open. I heard him curse when he discovered that I had not stopped in the wood. Then I heard their faint voices as they shouted to one another up and down the stream. That surprised me. I had thought of the stream, naturally, as a morning's march away.

I saw no more of the hunt. A few hours later there was a lot of splashing and excitement down by the water. They must have been dragging the pools for my body. The stream was a shallow mountain torrent, but quite fast enough to roll a man along with it until he was caught by rock or eddy.

In the evening I heard dogs, and felt really frightened. I

started to tremble, and knew pain again, aches and stabs and throbbings, all the symphony of pain, all my members fiddling away to the beat of my heart, on it or off it or half a bar behind. I had come back to life, thanks to that healing tree. The dogs might have found me, but their master, whoever he was, never gave them a chance. He wasn't wasting time by putting them on a trail that he could follow himself; he was casting up and down the stream.

When night fell I came down from my tree. I could stand, and, with the aid of two sticks, I could shuffle slowly forwards, flat-footed and stiff-legged. I could think, too. None of my mental activities for the past twenty-four hours might be called thinking. I had allowed my body to take charge. It knew far more about escaping and healing than I did.

I must try to make my behaviour intelligible. This confession — shall I call it? — is written to keep myself from brooding, to get down what happened in the order in which it happened. I am not content with myself. With this pencil and exercise-book I hope to find some clarity. I create a second self, a man of the past by whom the man of the present may be measured. Lest what I write should ever, by accident or intention, become public property, I will not mention who I am. My name is widely known. I have been frequently and unavoidably dishonoured by the banners and praises of the penny press.

This shooting trip of mine started, I believe, innocently enough. Like most Englishmen, I am not accustomed to enquire very deeply into motives. I dislike and disbelieve in cold-blooded planning, whether it be suggested of me or of anyone else. I remember asking myself when I packed the telescopic sight what the devil I wanted it for; but I just felt that it might come in handy.

It is undoubtedly true that I had been speculating – a curiosity that we all share – upon the methods of guarding a great man, and how they might be circumvented. I had a fortnight's sport in Poland, and then crossed the frontier for more. I began moving rather aimlessly from place to place, and as I found myself getting a little nearer to the House with each night's lodging I became obsessed by this idea of a sporting stalk. I have asked myself once or twice since why I didn't leave the rifle behind. I think the answer is that it wouldn't have been cricket.

Police protection is based upon the assumption that an assassin is a half-crazed idiot with a clumsy, close-range weapon – the bomb, the revolver, or the knife. It is obvious that the type of man who is a really fine shot and experienced in the approaching and killing of big-game would shrink from political or any other kind of murder. He probably hasn't any grievances, and, if he had, the rifle would not occur to him as a means of redressing them. I haven't any grievances myself. One can hardly count the upsetting of one's trivial private life and plans by European disturbances as a grievance. I don't see myself yowling of love like an Italian tenor and poking at the baritone with a stiletto.

A Bond Street rifle, I say, is not a weapon that the bodyguard need consider, for the potential assassin cannot train himself to use it. The secret police, who know all about the political antecedents of anyone disaffected to the régime, are not going to allow such a man to possess a good rifle, to walk about with it, or even to turn himself into a first-class shot. So the assassin is compelled to use a weapon that can be easily concealed.

Now, I argued, here am I with a rifle, with a permit to carry it, with an excuse for possessing it. Let us see whether, as an academic point, such a stalk and such a bag are possible. I went no further than that. I planned nothing. It has always been my habit to let things take their course.

I sent my baggage home by train, and covered the last hundred miles or so on foot, travelling only with a knapsack, my rifle and sight, my maps and my field-glasses. I marched by night. During daylight I lay up in timber or heath. I have never enjoyed anything so much. Whoever has stalked a beast for a couple of miles would understand what a superbly exciting enterprise it was to stalk over a hundred passing unseen through the main herds of human beings, the outliers, the young males walking unexpectedly upon hillsides. I was killing two birds with one stone; I revived in myself a sense of adventure and – well, I don't see why I wrote two birds. There was only one bird: the fun of the stalk.

I arrived on the ground at dawn and spent the whole day in reconnaissance. It was an alarming day, for the forest surrounding the House was most efficiently patrolled. From tree to tree and gully to gully I prowled over most of the circuit, but only flat on the earth was I really safe. Often I hid my rifle and glasses, thinking that I was certain to be challenged and questioned. I never was. I might have been transparent. I have learned the trick of watching shadows, and standing motionless in such a position that they cut and dapple my outline; still, there were times when even a rhinoceros could have seen me.

Here, at any rate, they had considered the offensive possibilities of the rifle. At all points commanding the terrace and the gardens clearings had been cut; nobody, even at extreme ranges, could shoot from cover. Open spaces, constantly crossed by guards, there were in plenty. I chose the narrowest of them: a ride some fifty feet broad which ran straight through the woods and ended at the edge of a low cliff. From the grass slope above the cliff the terrace and the doors leading on to it were in full sight. I worked out the range as five hundred and fifty yards.

I spent the night on a couch of pine needles, well hidden under the mother tree, and finished my provisions and slept undisturbed. A little before dawn I climbed a few feet down the cliff and squatted on a ledge where the overhang protected me from anyone who might peer over the brink. A stunted elder, clawing at the gravel with the tips of its top-heavy roots, was safe enough cover from distant eyes looking upwards. In that cramped position my rifle was useless, but I could, and very clearly, see the great man were he to come out and play with the dog or smell a rose or practise gestures on the gardener.

A path ran across the bottom of the ride, just above my head, and continued along the lower edge of the woods. I timed the intervals at which I heard footsteps, and discovered that somebody crossed the ride about every fourteen minutes. As soon as I was certain of that, I came out of hiding and followed. I wanted to understand his exact routine.

He was a young guard of splendid physique, with loyalty written all over him, but he had, I should think, hardly been out of an industrial town in his life. He couldn't have seen me if I had been under his feet. He knew perfectly well that he was not alone, for he looked over his shoulder again and again, and stared at the bush or the fold in the ground where I was; but of course he put his sensation down to nervousness or imagination. I treated him with disrespect, but I liked him; he was such a sturdy youth, with one of those fleshy open faces and the right instincts – a boy worth teaching. His eyes when he bagged his first tiger would be enough reward for putting up with a month of his naïve ideas.

After I had been round his beat with him and behind him, I knew for how many minutes, at any given time, I could occupy the grass slope, and by what route I must escape. When at last the great man came out to the terrace, my young friend had just passed. I had ten minutes to play with. I was up at once on to the slope.

I made myself comfortable, and got the three pointers of the sight steady on the V of his waistcoat. He was facing me and winding up his watch. He would never have known what shattered him – if I had meant to fire, that is. Just at that moment I felt a slight breeze on my cheek. It had been dead calm till then. I had to allow for the wind. No doubt the great man's disciples would see the hand of the Almighty in that. I should not disagree with them, for providence assuredly takes special care of any lone and magnificent male. Everyone who has stalked a particularly fine head knows that. It's natural enough. The Almighty Himself is always considered to be masculine.

I heard a yell. The next thing I knew was that I was coming round from a severe blow on the back of the head, and my young friend was covering me with his revolver. He had hurled a stone at me and himself after it – immediate, instinctive action far swifter than fiddling with his holster. We stared at each other. I remember complaining incoherently that he was seven minutes early. He looked at me as if I had been the devil in person, with horror, with fear – not fear of me, but fear at the suddenly revealed depravity of this world.

'I turned back,' he said. 'I knew.'

Well, of course he did. I should never have been such a conceited fool as to upset his nerves and his routine by following him about. He had neither heard me nor set eyes on me, but he was aware enough to make his movements irregular.

Together with his commanding officer he took me down to the House, and there, as I have already written, I was questioned by professionals. My captor left the room after disgracing his manhood – or so he thought – by being violently sick. Myself, I was detached. Perhaps I should not call it detachment, for my body is sensitive and there was no interruption or hiatus in its messages to my brain. But training counts.

I hold no brief for the pre-war Spartan training of the English upper class – or middle class as it is now the fashion to call it, leaving the upper to the angels – since in the ordinary affairs of a conventional life it is not of the slightest value to anyone; but it is of use on the admittedly rare occasions when one needs a high degree of physical endurance. I have been through an initiation ceremony on the Rio Javary – the only way I could persuade them to teach me how their men can exercise a slight muscular control over haemorrhage – and I thought it more a disagreeable experience than any proof of maturity. It lasted only a day and a night, whereas the initiation ceremonies of the tribal English continue for the ten years of education. We torture a boy's spirit rather than his body, but all torture is, in the end, directed at the spirit. I was conditioned to endure without making an ass of myself. That is all I mean by detachment.

I suspect that resignation was a lot easier for me than for a real assassin, since I had nothing at all to give away, no confederates, no motive. I couldn't save myself by telling them anything interesting. I had no right to endanger others by irresponsible invention. So I kept on automatically repeating the truth without the slightest hope that it would be believed.

At last someone recognized my name, and my story of a sporting stalk became faintly possible; but, whether it were true or not, it was now more than ever essential that I be discreetly murdered. And that was easy. I had admitted that I had not spent a night under a roof for five days, and that nobody knew where I was. They put all my papers and possessions back into my pockets, drove me fifty miles to the north, and staged the accident.

When I came down from that blessed larch and found that my legs would carry me, I began, I say, to look forward. It would be supposed either that I was drowned or that I was lying hurt and incapable in some riverside cover where my corpse would eventually be found. The police and the authorities in neighbouring villages would be warned to look out for a moribund stranger, but it was most unlikely that any description of me would have been circularized to other districts. The security offices at the House had no official knowledge of my existence and would share their unofficial knowledge with as few outsiders as possible. It was a convenience to have no existence. Had I stolen a watch instead of stalking the head of a nation my photograph would have been in all the police stations.

If I could walk, if I had new breeches, and if I could pass the danger zone without calling attention to myself, my chance of clearing out of the country was not negligible. I had my passport, my maps, and my money. I spoke the language well enough to deceive anyone but a highly educated man listening for mistakes. Dear old Holy George – my private nickname for their ambassador in London – insists that I speak a dialect, but to him polished grammar is more important than accent. That's a superstition inseparable from foreign affairs. A well-trained diplomat is supposed to write French, for example, like an angel, but to speak it with the peculiar gutlessness of a Geneva nancy-boy.

I wish I could apologize to Holy George. He had certainly spent some hours of those last twenty-four in answering very confidential cables about me – wiring as respectfully as possible that the bodyguard of his revered master were a pack of bloody fools, and following up with a strong letter to the effect that I was a member of his club and that it was unthinkable I should be mixed up in any such business as was, he could hardly believe seriously, suggested. I fear he must have been reprimanded. The bodyguard were, on the face of it, right.

It was now, I think, Sunday night; it was a Saturday when I was caught, but I am not sure of the lapse of time thereafter. I missed a day somewhere, but whether it was in my tree or on my island I cannot tell.

I knew roughly where I was, and that, to escape from this tumbled world of rock and forest, I should follow any path which ran parallel to the stream. My journey would not have been difficult if I had had crutches, but I could find no pieces of wood of the right height and with an angle to fit under the arm. It was, when I come to think of it, a nearly impossible quest, but at the time I was angry with myself, angry to the point when I wept childish tears of impotence. I couldn't make my hands use enough pressure on a knife, and I couldn't find sticks of the right length and shape. For an hour I raged and cursed at myself. I thought my spirit had altogether broken. It was pardonable. When everything was impossible, it was unreasonable to expect myself to distinguish between the miracle that could be forced to happen and the miracle that could not happen.

Finally, of course, I had to accept a miracle that could be

forced; to make myself progress without crutches. With a rough staff in each hand I managed about four miles, shuffling over even ground, and crawling for short distances over obstacles or for long distances whenever my legs become unbearably painful. I remember that common experience of carrying a heavy suitcase farther than it can reasonably be carried; one changes it from arm to arm at shorter and shorter intervals until one can no longer decide whether to continue the pain in the right or change to instant pain in the left. So it was with me in my changes from crawling to walking and back again.

I thanked God for the dawn, for it meant that I need not drive myself any farther. Until I knew exactly where I was, and upon what paths men came and went, I had to hide. I collapsed into a dry ditch and lay there for hours. I heard no sounds except a lark and the crunch of cows tearing at the grass in a neighbouring field.

At last I stood up and had a look at my surroundings. I was near the top of a ridge. Below me and to the left was the wooded valley along which I had come. I had not noticed in the night that I was climbing. Part of my exhaustion had been due to the rising ground.

I shuffled upwards to the skyline. The long curve of a river was spread out at my feet. The near bank was clothed in low bushes through which ran a footpath, appearing and disappearing until it crossed the mouth of my stream by an iron bridge. On the farther bank, a mile upstream, was a country town with a few small factories. Downstream there were pastures on both banks and a small islet in the centre of the river. It was tranquil and safe as any of our hidden English Avons.

I got out the map and checked my position. I was looking at a tributary which, after a course of thirty miles, ran into one of the main rivers of Europe. From this town, a provincial capital, the search for me would be directed, and to it the police, my would-be rescuers, presumably belonged. Nevertheless I had to go there. It was the centre of communications: road, river and railway. And since I could not walk I had to find some transport to carry me to the frontier.

At intervals the breeze bore to me the faint sound of cries and splashing. I thought someone was being hurt – a morbid fancy, natural enough in the circumstances – but then I realized that the screaming was the collective voice of several women, and that they were bathing. It occurred to me that when commerce and education stopped for lunch men might come to swim at the same place, and I could lay my hands on a pair of trousers.

I waited until I saw the girls cross the iron footbridge on their way back to town, and then hobbled down the ridge – a stony, barren hillside where there were, thank heaven, no fences to cross and no officious small-holder to ask me what I was doing. The bathing-place was plain enough, a semi-circle of grass with a clean drop of three feet into the river. Above and below it the bank was covered with a dense growth of willow and alder. I took to my elbows and belly again, and crawled into the thicket. There was already a sort of runway leading into it, which, at the time, I could only assume the Lord had made for my special benefit. I realized afterwards that it had been bored through the bushes by some young fellow who was curious to know the female form and too poor to arrange for it in the ordinary way. I think of him as charitably as I can. From the end of his burrow I had an excellent view of the bushes behind which a modest bather would undress.

My necessary males were not long in coming. Indeed I had

a narrow shave, for I heard them yelling and singing their way along the path before I had turned myself round. They were five hefty lads: sons, I should think, of shopkeepers and petty officials. There were two pairs of shorts, two nondescript trousers, and an old pair of riding-breeches. For my build all had the waistbands too roomy and the legs too short, and I couldn't guess which pair would best fit me. It was that, I think, which gave me the brilliant idea of taking them all. To steal one pair of trousers would obviously direct attention to some passing tramp or fugitive; but if all disappeared, the theft would be put down as the practical joke of a comrade. I remember chuckling crazily as I worked my way back to the edge of the bushes.

They undressed in the open, ten yards from the water. That meant there was only one chance for me – to do the job the moment the last man had dived in and before the first came out. It was a mad risk, but I had gone long beyond caring what risks I took.

They dived in within a few seconds of each other, all but one who remained on the bank shadow-boxing with his fat-bottomed, idiotic self until a friend, as fed up with his posing as I was, reached an arm for his ankles and pulled him in. I was out of my observation post on the instant and hunching myself across the grass. I got four pairs; the fifth was too far away. I just had time to slip behind a bramble bush before one of them pulled himself up the bank. He didn't look at the clothes – why should he? – and I crawled downstream with the trousers.

Now what was the one place where they would not look? To climb a second tree was unsafe; young men in high spirits naturally think of trees. As for the bushes, they would trample them down like a herd of buffalo. The best place for me was, I decided, the water. No one would expect a practical joker, presumably fully dressed, to go to such lengths as to sink himself and his friends' breeches in the river. I made for the bank and slid under the willows into a patch of still water full of scum and brushwood. Two of them were swimming quite close, but the boughs trailing in the water protected me well enough from casual glances.

I needn't have taken so much trouble, for the plan succeeded more easily than I dared hope. They dashed up the path, and I heard their voices resounding from the hillside as they yelled for one Willy. When Willy was not to be found, they draped towels round the tails of their shirts and stormed through the thicket. I don't know if they actually looked over the bank where I was. I heard one of them within a yard or two, and ducked. At last, in an evil mood, they took the path for home and Willy. They never doubted for a moment that the culprit was Willy. I hope they didn't believe his denials till he was thoroughly punished. The sort of man whom one instantly accuses of any practical joke that has been played deserves whatever is coming to him.

Together with the trousers I let myself float down to the islet which I had seen from the top of the ridge. I could only use my arms for swimming. My generation never normally learned the crawl, and my old-fashioned frog's leg-stroke was too painful to be possible. However, I managed to keep myself and my soggy raft of trousers well out into the river, and the current did the rest.

The islet was bare, but with enough low vegetation on its shores to cover me, provided I kept close to the edge, from observation by anyone on the high ground where I had lain that morning. There were four notices, neatly spaced, to the effect that it was forbidden to land. I can't conceive why.

Perhaps because any idle person in a boat would naturally want to land, and anything that encourages idleness is considered immoral.

I spread out myself, my clothes, and the breeches to dry in the afternoon sun. I did not attempt to examine my body. It was enough that the soaking had separated textile from flesh with no worse result than a gentle oozing of matter.

I remained on the islet for the Monday night and all the following day. Probably I was there for the Tuesday night too. I do not know; as I say, I lost a day somewhere. It was very heavenly, for I lay on the sand naked and undisturbed, and allowed the sun to start the work of healing. I was barely conscious most of the time. I would hunch myself into the half-shade of the weeds and rushes and sleep till I grew cold, and I would hunch myself back again and roast and scar my wounds. I had but those two pleasures within attaining, and both were utterly satisfying. I did not want food. I was, I suppose, running a fever, so my lack of appetite was natural. I did suffer from the cold at night, but not severely. I had all the various garments to cover me, and, at any other time, I should have thought the weather too hot and still for easy sleep.

I awoke, feeling clear-headed and ravenously hungry, at the false dawn of what turned out to be Wednesday. I chose the riding-breeches – holding them against my body they seemed roomy enough not to rub my hide – and threw shorts and trousers into the river. I hope that their small change was not too great a loss to the owners. Only one had a wallet, and that, since it stuck out from his hip-pocket, I had managed to slip on top of the rest of his clothes.

I tied two bits of driftwood together with my belt, and put all my possessions on this improvised raft. I found that I could splash with more ease – though the regular motions of swimming were still beyond me – and reached the farther bank, the raft helping, without being carried more than a hundred yards downstream.

On dry land and within a stone's throw of a main road, I had to take stock of my appearance. So far my looks had mattered no more to me than the condition of its fur to an animal; but now I proposed to re-enter the world of men, and the impression I made was vitally important. Only my shoes and stockings were respectable. I couldn't bend to take them off, so the river had cleaned them.

Item: I had to shave off a four days' beard. That was far from being the mere prejudice of an Englishman against appearing in public with his bristles. If a man is clean shaved and has a well-fitting collar and tie – even reasonably dirty – he can get away with a multitude of suspicious circumstances.

Item: Gloves. The ends of my fingers had to be shown while paying money and taking goods, and they were not human.

Item: An Eyeshade. My left eye was in a condition that could not be verified without a mirror. The eyelid had stuck to a mess of what I hoped was only blood.

Item: A Clothes Brush. My tweed coat had no elbows, but it might pass provided I brushed off the mud and did not turn away from anyone I spoke to.

I had to have these things. Without them I might as well have given myself up. I had not the will to crawl and hobble night after night to the frontier, nor the agility to steal enough to eat; but if I entered so much as a village shop as I was, the proprietor would promptly escort me to the police or a hospital.

The putting-on of the breeches was an interminable agony. When at last I had them up, I couldn't fasten the blasted buttons. I managed three and had to forgo the rest for fear of leaving bloodstains all over the cloth. Shirt buttons were quite impossible.

I crossed a field and stood for a moment on the empty main road. It was the hour before dawn, the sky an imperial awning fringed with blue and gold. The tarred surface of the road was blue and calm as a canal. Only the trains were alive, dashing across the flat vale as if striving to reach the mountains before day. At my disposal, as the map had told me, were river, road, and railway. I was inclined to favour escape by river. A man drifting down the current in a boat doesn't have to answer questions or fill up forms. But again there was the insuperable handicap of my appearance. I couldn't present myself as I was to buy a boat, and if I stole one and it were missed, my arrest was certain at the next village down-river.

On the far side of the road was a farm-cart, backed against the edge of a field of wheat. I knelt behind it to watch the passers-by. Men were already stirring, a few peasants in the fields, a few walkers on the road. From the latter I hoped to obtain help, or at least, by observing them, an inspiration how to help myself.

There was a workman bound for some small factory in the town to whom I nearly spoke. He had an honest, kindly face – but so have most of them. I had no reason at all to suppose he would protect me. Two aimless wanderers went by together. They looked to be persons who would sympathize, but their faces were those of scared rabbits. I couldn't trust them. Then there were several peasants on their way to the fields. I could only pray that they wouldn't enter mine. They would have had some sport with me before handing me over to the police; they seemed that sort. There was a wretched fellow mumbling and weeping, who raised my hopes for a moment. But misery is in some way as sacred as happiness; one doesn't intrude – not, at any rate, if there is a risk that one might merely add to the misery. Then came another factory-worker, and then a tall, stooping man with a fishing rod. He cut across to the river and began to fish not far from where I had landed. He had a melancholy, intellectual face with a deal of strength in it, and I decided to have another look at him.

Their tiresome conception of the State has one comforting effect; it creates so many moral lepers that no one of them, if he has a little patience, can long be lonely. The flotsam of the nation is washed together into an unrecognized, nameless, formless secret society. There isn't much that the bits of scum can do to help one another, but at least they can cling and keep silence. And dawn, I think, is the hour when the pariah goes out. Not for him is the scornful morning with its crowds pointing the fingers of their minds at him, nor the evening when all but he may rest and be merry; but the peace before sunrise cannot be taken from him. It is the hour of the outlawed, the persecuted, the damned, for no man was ever born who could not feel some shade of hope if he were in open country with the sun about to rise. I did not formulate these thoughts at the time. I have developed them in the curious and lonely circumstances under which I write. But I give them for what they are worth to account for my intuition in choosing the right face and the fact that there were so many to choose from.

There was no cover on the farther side of the road and precious little on the bank, so that I had to make up my mind about the fisherman as I slowly and silently crossed the field towards him. He was paying more attention to his thoughts than to his rod. By the angle of his float I could see that he had hooked the bottom, but he was quite unaware of it. I walked up behind him and wished him good morning and asked if he had had any luck. He jumped to his feet with the butt of the rod pointed towards me as if to keep me off. I expect he hadn't seen a creature like me in a long time; they haven't any tramps. Even considering me the last word in villains, he thought it best to propitiate me. He apologized for his fishing, and said he didn't think there was anything wrong in it. He did his best to look servile, but his eyes burned with courage.

I held out my hands to him and asked if he knew how that was done. He didn't answer a word, just waited for further information.

'Look here!' I said to him, 'I swear there isn't a soul in this country who knows I am alive except yourself. I want gloves, shaving tackle, and a clothes brush. Don't buy them. Give me old things that have no mark on them by which they could be traced back to you if I am caught. And if you don't mind putting your hand in my inside coat-pocket you will find money.'

'I don't want money,' he said.

His face was absolutely expressionless. He wasn't giving anything away. He might have meant that he wouldn't help a fugitive for all the money in the world, or that he wouldn't take money for helping a fugitive. The next move was up to me.

'Do you speak English?' I asked.

I saw a flicker of interest in his eyes, but he made no sign that he had understood me. I carried on in English. I was completely in his power, so that there was no point in hiding my nationality. I hoped that the foreign tongue might break down his reserve.

'I won't tell you who I am or what I have done,' I said, 'because it is wiser that you shouldn't know. But so long as no one sees us talking together, I don't think you run the slightest risk in helping me.'

'I'll help you,' he answered in English. 'What was it you wanted?'

I repeated my requirements and asked him to throw in an eye-patch and some food if he could manage it. I also told him that I was a rich man and he shouldn't hesitate to take any money he might need. He refused – with a very sweet, melancholy smile – but gave me an address in England to which I was to pay what I thought fit if ever I got home.

'Where shall I put the things?' he asked.

'Under the cart over there,' I answered. 'And don't worry. I shall be in the wheat, and I'll take care not to be seen.'

He said good-bye and moved off abruptly. In one stride he had dissociated himself from me completely. He knew by experience that among the proscribed the truest courtesy was to waste no time in courtesy.

The traffic on the road was increasing, and I had to wait some minutes before I could safely cross into the shelter of the wheat. The sun rose and the landscape budded men and business – barges on the river, a battalion out for a route march on the road, and damned, silent bicycles sneaking up every time I raised my head.

The fisherman was back in an hour, but the road was too busy for him to drop a parcel under the cart unseen. He solved the problem by fetching his rod and sitting on the cart while he took it apart and packed it. When he got up he accidentally left the parcel behind.

To get possession of it was the devil of a job, for I could not see what was about to pass until the traffic was nearly opposite me. I knelt in the wheat, bobbing my head up and down like a pious old woman divided between silent prayer and the responses. At last I plucked up courage and reached the cart. A stream of cars went by, but they did not matter; the danger was a pedestrian or a cyclist who might be tempted to stop and talk. I kept my back to the road and pretended to be tinkering with the axle. A woman wished me good morning, and that was the worst fright I had had since they pushed me over the cliff. I answered her surlily and she passed on. To wait for a clear road was exasperating, but I needed a full minute free from possible observation. I couldn't plunge boldly back into the wheat. I had to tread gently, separating the stalks so as not to leave too obvious a track behind me.

At last I knelt in peace and unpacked the parcel which that blessed fisherman had left for me. There were a bottle of milk well laced with brandy, bread and the best part of a cold chicken. He had thought of everything, even hot shaving-water in a thermos flask.

When I had finished his food I felt equal to looking in the mirror. I was cleaner than I expected; the morning swim was responsible for that. But I didn't recognize myself. It was not the smashed eye which surprised me – that was merely closed, swollen and ugly. It was the other eye. Glaring back at me from the mirror, deep and enormous, it seemed to belong to someone intensely alive, so much more alive than I felt. My face was all pallors and angles, like that of a Christian martyr in a medieval painting – and I had the added villainy of bristles. I marvelled how such a beastly crop could grow in so poor and spiritual a soil.

I put on my gloves – limp leather, God reward him, and several sizes too large! – then shaved, brushed my clothes, and dressed myself more tidily. My coat and shirt were patterned in shades of brown, and the blood stains, weakened by my swim to the island, hardly showed. When I had cleaned up and adjusted the eye-patch, I came to the conclusion that I aroused pity rather than suspicion. I looked like a poor but educated man, a clerk or schoolmaster, convalescent after some nasty accident. That was evidently the right part to play.

As soon as I was ready I left the wheat, for now I did not care how wide a track I made so long as no one actually saw me emerge. The road was clearer; it had ceased to feed and empty the town, and become an artery in a greater life. Lorries and cars sped by with the leisurely roar of through traffic. Their drivers had no neighbourly feelings towards that mile of road, no damned curiosity about a lonely pedestrian. I covered the mile into town, limping along as best I could and stopping frequently to rest. At need I could walk very slowly and correctly, hanging on each foot, as if waiting for somebody.

I was desperately nervous when first I engaged myself between two lines of houses. There seemed to be so many windows observing me, such crowds on the streets. Looking back on it, I cannot think that I passed more than a score of people, mostly women shopping; but, at the best of times, I have a tendency to agoraphobia. Even in London I avoid crowds at all cost; to push my way through the drift of suburban idlers in Oxford Street is torment to me. The streets of that town were really no more full nor empty than those of my own country town, and normally I should not have been affected; but I seemed to have been out of human society for years.

I cut down to the river by the first turning, and came out on to a paved walk, with flower-beds and a bandstand, where I could stroll at my artificial pace without making myself conspicuous. Ahead, under the bridge, were moored a dozen boats. When I came abreast of them I saw the expected notice of 'Boats for Hire' in a prettily painted cottage. There was a man leaning on the fence, meditative and unbuttoned, and obviously digesting his breakfast while mistaking that process for thought.

I wished him good day and asked if I could hire a boat. He looked at me suspiciously and remarked that he had never seen me before, as if that ended the discussion. I explained that I was a schoolmaster recovering from a motor accident and had been ordered by my doctor to spend a week in the open air. He took his pipe out of his mouth and said that he didn't hire boats to strangers. Well, had he one for sale? No, he had not. So there we were. He evidently didn't like the look of me and wasn't going to argue.

A shrill yell came from a bedroom window:

'Sell him the punt, idiot!'

I looked up. A red face and formidable bust were hanging over the window-sill, both quivering with exasperation. I bowed to her with the formality of a village teacher, and she came down.

'Sell him what he wants, dolt!' she ordered.

Her small, screaming voice came most oddly from so huge a bulk. I imagine he had driven her voice higher and higher with impatience until it stuck permanently on its top note.

'I don't know who he is,' insisted her husband with stupid surliness.

'Well, who are you?' she shrieked, as if I had repeatedly refused her the information.

I told my story: how I couldn't yet walk with any ease, and so had thought of spending a holiday in drifting down the river from town to town and realizing a dream of my youth.

'Where's your baggage?' asked that damned boatman.

I patted my pockets, bulging with the thermos flask and shaving tackle. I told him I needed no more than a nightshirt and a tooth-brush.

That set the old girl off again. She skirled like a sucking-pig separated from the litter.

'You expect him to travel with a trunk? He's a proper man, not an ignorant, shameless idler who wastes good money on clubs and uniforms and whores, and would rather go to the river than raise his hand to pull the plug. He shall have his boat! And cheap!'

She stamped down to the waterfront and showed me the punt. It was comfortable, but far too long and clumsy to be handled by a man who couldn't sit to paddle. It wasn't cheap. She asked about double its fair price. Evidently her kindness was not at all disinterested.

There was a twelve-foot dinghy with a red sail, and I enquired if it was for sale. She said it was too expensive for me.

'I shall sell it again wherever I finish the trip.' I answered. 'And I have a little money – compensation for my accident.'

She made her husband step the mast and hoist the sail. How that man hated the pair of us! He announced with gusto that I should certainly drown myself and that his wife would take the blame. A child couldn't have drowned himself. That boat was exactly what I wanted. The sail was hardly more than a toy, but it would be a considerable help with the wind astern, and was not large enough to be a hindrance if I let go the sheet and drifted with the current. I knew that some days must pass before I felt equal to the effort of tacking.

While she raved at her husband, I got out my wallet. I didn't want them to see how much I had, nor to wonder at my fumbling with gloved hands.

'There!' I said, holding out to her a sheaf of notes. 'That's all I can afford. Tell me yes or no.'

I don't know whether it was less or more than she

intended to ask, but it was a sight more than the little tub was worth to anyone but me. She looked astonished at my rural simplicity and began to haggle, just for form's sake. I sympathized; I said that no doubt she was right, but that sum was all I could pay for a boat. She took it, of course, and gave me a receipt. In five minutes I was out on the river, and they were wondering, I suppose, why the crazy schoolmaster should kneel on the bottom-boards instead of sitting on a thwart, and why he didn't have his coat decently mended.

Of the days and nights that passed on the tributary and the main river there is little to write. I was out of any immediate danger, and content – far more content than I am now, though no less solitary. I didn't exist, and so long as I was not compelled to show my papers there was no reason why I should exist. Patience was all I needed, and easy enough to keep. I recovered my strength as peacefully as if I had been the convalescent I pretended; indeed, thinking myself into the part actually helped me to recover. I nearly believed in my motor accident, my elementary school, my housekeeper, and my favourite pupils about whom I prattled when I fell in with other users of the river or when I took a meal in an obscure riverside tavern.

From nightfall to dawn I moored my boat in silent reaches of the river, choosing high or marshy or thickly wooded banks where no one could burst in upon me with questions. At first I had taken to the ditches and backwaters, but the danger of that amphibian habit was impressed on me when a farmer led his horses down to drink in my temporary harbour, and insisted on regarding me as a suspicious character. Rain was the greatest hardship I had to endure. After a night's soaking I felt the chill of the morning mist. A rubber sheet was unobtainable, but I managed at last to buy a tarpaulin. It kept me dry and uncomfortably warm, but it was heavy, and hard for my hands to fold and unfold. Only the most persistent rain could force me to use it.

I made but sixty miles in the first week. My object was to heal myself rather than hurry. I took no risks and expended no effort. Until the back of my thighs had grown some sturdy scars I had to kneel while sailing or drifting, and lie on my stomach across the thwarts while sleeping. That limited my speed. I could not row.

In the second week I tried to buy an outboard motor, and only just got out of the deal in time. I found that to purchase an engine and petrol I had to sign enough papers to ensure my arrest by every political or administrative body that had heard of me. I must say, they have made the way of the transgressor uncommonly difficult. At the next town, however, there was an old-fashioned yard where I bought a business-like lugsail and had a small foresail fitted into the bargain. Thereafter I carried my own stores, and never put in to town or village. With my new canvas and the aid of the current I could sometimes do forty miles a day, and – what was more important – could keep out of the way of the barges and tugs that were now treating the river as their own.

All the way down-river I had considered the problem of my final escape from the country, and had arrived at three possible solutions. The first was to keep on sailing and trust to luck. This was obviously very risky, for only a fast motorboat could slip past the patrol craft off the port. I should be turned back, either as a suspicious character or an ignorant idiot who oughtn't to be allowed in a boat – and the chances, indeed, were against my little twelve-foot tub being able to live in the short, breaking seas of the estuary.

The second plan was to embark openly on a passenger vessel – or train, for that matter – and trust that my name and description had never been circularized to the frontier police.

This, earlier, I might have tried if I had had the strength; but as my voyage crept into its third week it seemed probable that even the most extensive search for my body would have been abandoned, that it would be assumed I was alive, and that every blessed official was praying for a sight of me and promotion.

My third solution was to hang around the docks for an opportunity of stowing away or stealing a boat or seeing a yacht which belonged to some friend. But this demanded time – and I could neither sleep in a hotel without being invited to show my papers to a lodging-house keeper, nor in the open without showing them to a policeman. Whatever I did, I had to do immediately after arrival at the port.

Now, of course I was thinking stupidly. The way out of the country was laughably easy. A boy who had merely hit a policeman would have thought of it at once. But in my mind I was a convalescent schoolmaster or I was a ghost. I had divested myself of my nationality and forgotten that I could call on the loyalty of my compatriots. I had nearly thrown away my British passport on the theory that no papers whatever would be safer than my own. As soon as I came in sight of the wharves, I saw British ships and realized that I had merely to tell a good enough story to the right man to be taken aboard.

I moored my boat to a public landing-stage and went ashore. I made a bad mistake in not sinking her; it did occur to me that I should, but, quite apart from the nuisance of sailing back up the river to find a quiet spot where she could be sunk unobserved, I disliked the thought of the friendly little country tub rotting away at the disgusting bottom of an industrial river.

I bought myself a nondescript outfit of blue serge at the first slop-shop I came to, and changed in a public lavatory.

My old clothes I sold in another slop-shop – that seeming the best way to get rid of them without a trace. If ever they were bought it must have been by the poorest of workmen. He'll find an unexpected bargain in my favourite coat; it will last him all his life.

Strolling along the quays, I got into conversation with two British seamen by means of the old and tried introduction (which has extracted many a sixpence from me) – 'Got a match?' We had a drink together. Neither of them were in ships bound for England, but they had a pal in a motorship which was sailing for London the next day.

The pal, hailed from the bar to join us on our bench, was a bit wary of me; he was inclined to think that I was a parson from the seamen's mission masquerading as an honest worker. I calmed his suspicions with two double whiskies and my most engaging dirty story, whereupon he declared that I was a Bit of All Right and consented to talk about his officers. The captain, it seemed, was a stickler for correct detail – thinks 'e'll lose 'is ticket if 'e forgets a muckin' 'alfpenny stamp. But Mr Vaner, the First Officer, was a One and a Fair Caution; I gathered from his wry smile that the pal found the mate a hard taskmaster, while admiring his flamboyant character. Mr Vaner was obviously the man for me. And yes, I might catch him still on board if I hurried because he had been out late the night before.

She was a little ship, hardly more than a coaster, lying alongside an endless ribbon of wharf with her grey and white forecastle nosing up towards the load-line of the huge empty tramp in front of her, like a neat fox-terrier making the acquaintance of a collie.

Two dock policemen were standing near by. I kept my back to them while I hailed the deck importantly.

'Mr Vaner on board?'

The cook, who was peeling potatoes on a hatch-cover, looked up from the bucket between his knees.

'I'll see, sir.'

That 'sir' was curious and comforting. In spite of my shabby foreign clothing and filthy shoes, the cook had placed me at a glance in Class X. He would undoubtedly describe me as a gent, and Mr Vaner would feel he ought to see me.

I say Class X because there is no definition of it. To talk of an upper or a ruling class is nonsense. The upper class, if the term has any meaning at all, means landed gentry who probably do belong to Class X but form only a small proportion of it. The ruling class are, I presume, politicians and servants of the State – terms which are self-contradictory.

I wish there were some explanation of Class X. We are politically a democracy – or should I say that we are an oligarchy with its ranks ever open to talent? – and the least class-conscious of nations in the Marxian sense. The only class-conscious people are those who would like to belong to Class X and don't: the suburban old-school-tie brigade and their wives, especially their wives. Yet we have a profound division of classes which defies analysis since it is in a continual state of flux.

Who belongs to Class X? I don't know till I talk to him and then I know at once. It is not, I think, a question of accent, but rather of the gentle voice. It is certainly not a question of clothes. It may be a question of bearing. I am not talking, of course, of provincial society in which the division between gentry and non-gentry is purely and simply a question of education.

I should like some socialist pundit to explain to me why it is that in England a man can be a member of the proletariat by every definition of the proletariat (that is, by the nature of his employment and his poverty) and yet obviously belong to Class X, and why another can be a bulging capitalist or cabinet minister or both and never get nearer to Class X than being directed to the Saloon Bar if he enters the Public.

I worry with this analysis in the hope of hitting on some new method of effacing my identity. When I speak a foreign language I can disguise my class, background, and nationality without effort, but when I speak English to an Englishman I am at once spotted as a member of X. I want to avoid that, and if the class could be defined I might know how.

Mr Vaner received me in his cabin. He was a dashing young man in his early twenties, with his cap on the back of a head of brown curls. His tiny stateroom was well hung with feminine photographs, some cut from the illustrated week-lies, some personally presented and inscribed in various languages. He evidently drove himself hard on land as well as sea.

As soon as we had shaken hands, he said:

'Haven't met you before, have I?'

'No. I got your name from one of the hands. I hear you are sailing tomorrow.'

'Well?' he asked guardedly.

I handed him my passport.

'Before we go any further, I want you to satisfy yourself that I am British and really the person I pretend to be.'

He looked at my passport, then up at my face and eyeshade.

'That's all right,' he said. 'Take a seat, won't you? You seem to have been in trouble, sir.'

'I have, by God! And I want to get out of it.'

'A passage? If it depended on me, but I'm afraid the old man . . .'

I told him that I didn't want a passage, that I wouldn't put so much responsibility on either him or the captain; all I wanted was a safe place to stow away.

He shook his head and advised me to try a liner.

'I daren't risk it,' I answered. 'But show me where to hide, and I give you my word of honour that no one shall see me during the voyage or when I go ashore.'

'You had better tell me a little more,' he said.

He threw himself back in his chair and cocked one leg over the other. His face assumed a serious and judicial air, but his delightfully swaggering pose showed that he was enjoying himself.

I spun him a yarn which, so far as it went, was true. I told him that I was in deadly trouble with the authorities, that I had come down the river in a boat, and that an appeal to our consul was quite useless.

'I might put you in the store-room,' he said doubtfully. 'We're going home in ballast, and there's nowhere in the hold for you to hide.'

I suggested that the store-room was too dangerous, that I didn't want to take the remotest chance of being seen and getting the ship into trouble. That seemed to impress him.

'Well,' he replied, 'if you can stand it, there's an empty freshwater tank which we never use, and I could prop up the cover so that you'd get some air. But I expect that you've slept in worse places, sir, now that I come to think of it.'

'You recognized my name?'

'Of course. I wouldn't do this for anyone.'

All the same I think he would, given a story that appealed to him.

I asked when I could come aboard.

'No time like the present! I don't know who's down in the engine-room, but there's nobody on deck except the cook. I'll just deal with the cops!'

He waited till the couple of police had walked two hundred yards up the wharf and then started waving and shouting good-bye as if someone had just gone away between the warehouses. The two looked round and continued their stroll; they had no reason to doubt that a visitor left the ship while they had their backs to her.

Mr Vaner sent the cook ashore to buy a bottle of whisky.

'You'll need something to mix with your water,' he chuckled, immensely pleased that he had now committed himself to the adventure, 'and I don't want him around while I open up the tank. You wait here and make yourself comfortable.'

I asked him what I had better say if anyone came aboard unexpectedly and found me in his cabin.

'Say? Oh, tell 'em you're her father!' He pointed to a photograph of a giggling young girl who was bashfully displaying her legs as if to advertise silk stockings. 'I should surely have urgent business elsewhere if you were. Inside the water tank myself, as likely as not!'

He settled his cap over one ear and marched out of the cabin, whistling with such an elaborate air of unconcern that any one of his young women would have known he was planning some deception. But I was pretty sure he would take no risks. His play-acting was for his own amusement and for me, his partner in crime. To the rest of the world he was the responsible ship's officer.

He was back in ten minutes.

'Hurry!' he said. 'The cops have just gone round the corner.'

We did have to hurry. The manhole was on a level with and in full view of the wharf, being set into the quarterdeck between the after wall of the chart-room and a lifeboat slung athwart ship. We took a hasty look round and I pushed myself through into a space about the size of half a dozen coffins.

'I'll make you comfortable later on,' he said. 'It will be slack water in about two hours.'

I was comfortable enough, more relaxed than I had been since the first week on the river. The darkness and the six walls gave me an immediate sense of safety. I had gone to ground after the hunt, and the cold iron of the closed tank was more protective than the softest grass in the open. This was the first of my dens, and I think that it provided me with the idea of the second.

At the bottom of the ebb, when the quarter-deck had sunk well below the edge of the wharf, Mr Vaner turned up with blankets, the cushion of a settee, water, whisky, biscuits, and a covered bucket for my personal needs.

'Snug as a bug in a rug!' he declared cheerfully. 'And what's more, I've given you a safety-valve.'

'How's that?'

'I've disconnected the outflow. Can you see light?'

I looked down a small pipe at the bottom of the tank and did see light.

'That's on the wall of the captain's bathroom,' he said. 'I never knew we could get fresh water there. The worst of these labour-saving ships is that one never has time to find out all the gadgets. Now, you have that and you have the air intake, so if the old man notices the manhole and I have to screw it up for a time, you'll be all right.'

'Where do you dock?' I asked.

'We're going right up the river to Wandsworth. I'll tell you when it's safe to slip ashore.'

I heard steps on the deck – one heard in that tank everything that touched or struck the deck – and Mr Vaner disappeared. I never saw him again.

I dozed uneasily until all the noises ceased; the crew, I suppose, had come on board and settled down for the night. Then I slept in good earnest and awoke to the sound of heavy boots trampling above and below me; it was morning, for I could see light at the end of my two pipes. The manhole was screwed up tight with a finality which I didn't enjoy – not that there was the slightest risk of asphyxiation, but it suddenly occurred to me that if Mr Vaner were washed overboard I should be in the tank until the captain discovered, if he ever did discover, that he could fill his bath with fresh water by making a simple connexion. That was the sort of ridiculous fear which alcohol can dispel quicker than self-control, so I poured myself a stiff whisky and ate some biscuits.

Then we sailed – an unmistakable jangle of sounds like a hundred iron monkeys playing tag in a squash-court. Some hours later my manhole was opened and propped, and a cold mutton chop, with a note attached to it instead of a frill, descended on my stomach. I ate the chop and knelt below the crack of light to read the message.

'Sorry I had to screw you down. The cops found a boat and traced it to you. They turned us inside out this morning and all other ships at the wharf. Caught four stowaways, I hear. We are outside territorial waters, so you're OK. They know all about your eyeshade. If you're likely to run into any trouble, take it off. I'll slip you a pair of dark glasses when it's time to go. Dock police reported that a chap of your build had come on board and left. I said I had been asked for a passage, and refused. If you have any papers you want to get rid of, leave them in the tank and I'll deliver them wherever you direct.

R. Vaner (First Officer)

PS. Try not to upset anything. Have just remembered that if you do, it will run into the old man's bathroom.'

I wish I could have given the dashing Mr Vaner some convincing evidence that he was serving his country instead of a – well, I can't call myself a criminal. If there were any crimes committed, they were committed on my person. But, as I say, I do not blame them. They had every reason to think they had caught an assassin.

Their police organization is superb; but the finding of that paralysed thing which had crawled and bled was a casual job for foresters. Only within the last day or two, I expect, when an exhaustive search for my corpse at last suggested that there might be no corpse to find, did the House extend enquiries to road, rail, and river, and learn about the boating schoolmaster who had an eyeshade and always kept on his gloves. Then the police came into action. They hadn't picked me up, I should guess, for the simple reason that they had just begun to look for a boat with red sails and happened to miss the little yard where I changed them; but when some official noticed an unfamiliar dinghy moored where I probably had no right to moor her, she was at once identified.

Vaner's suggestion that my troubles might by no means be over when I reached London was disturbing. I hadn't given the matter any thought. One's instinct is against looking too far forward when the present demands all available resource.

I began to speculate on what would happen if I reappeared quite openly in England. I was perfectly certain that they would not appeal to the Foreign Office or to Scotland Yard. Whatever I might have done or intended, their treatment of me wouldn't stand publicity. They couldn't be sure how the English would react; nobody ever is. After all, we once went to war for the ear of a Captain Jenkins – though Jenkins was an obscurer person than myself and had, considering the number of laws he broke, been treated with no great barbarity.

Would they, then, follow me up themselves? Mr Vaner, with his taste for romance, appeared to think they would. I myself had assumed that once I was over the frontier, bygones would be bygones. I now saw that this was a foolishly optimistic view. They couldn't go to the police, true, but nor could I. I had committed an extraditable offence; if I complained of being molested, I might force them into telling why I was molested.

It came to this: I was an outlaw in my own country as in theirs, and if my death were required it could easily be accomplished. Even assuming they couldn't fake an accident or suicide, no motive or a wrong motive would be discovered for the crime, and no murderer or the wrong murderer would be arrested.

Then I thought that I had let myself be carried away by a casual phrase of Vaner's, and that this uneasiness was preposterous. Why on earth, I argued, should they take the unnecessary risk of removing me in my own country? Did they imagine that I was likely to put the wind up them by another of these sporting expeditions?

I reluctantly admitted that they might very well imagine it. They knew that I was an elusive person who could quite possibly return, if he chose, and upset the great man's nerves once more. As to whether I would so choose, there were among my opponents – I can't call them enemies – some notable big-game shots who would realize that the temptation was not unthinkable.

The manhole was never screwed up again, and I lay on my cushion suffering little more discomfort than I generally suffer at sea. I am a good sailor, but even in a first-class state-room I feel gently and sleepily bilious, disinclined to do more than walk from my cabin to the library and back, or be faintly polite to a fellow passenger at the hour of the aperitif. On the credit side of this voyage was the fact that I hadn't got to be polite to anyone; on the debit, that I hadn't got a book. I passed my time in sleep and slightly nightmarish meditation.

The boom and thump of the Diesels, resonant and regular as distant tribal drums, signalled to me our progress up the Thames. They slowed to pick up the pilot; they were fussed and flurried by the engine-room telegraph in the crowded waters of Gravesend Reach; they handed over to the whir of electric capstans when we tied up, as I guess, somewhere below bridges (for she rode too high to pass up-river on the top of the flood); they beat slowly seven hours later, while I imagined them carrying us up through the Pool and the City, through Westminster and Chelsea, until the telegraph belled them into incoherent rhythms and finished with the engines.

There were bangings and tramplings, and then silence. After a while my tank settled over to port, and I assumed that we were resting on the Wandsworth mud. Another note was dropped through the manhole, accompanied by a pair of formidably dark glasses wrapped in brown paper.

'Don't go out through the gates. There's a chap watching I don't like the look of. The dinghy is under the starboard quarter. As soon as she floats I'll give you a knock, and you beat it quick. Row across to the public steps by Hurlingham east wall. I'll take the boat back later. Best of luck.

R. VANER (First Officer)'

He rapped on the manhole an hour or so later, and I pushed

out my arms and shoulders by merely standing up; indeed I could stand up no other way. There was a light in Mr Vaner's cabin and a loud noise of conversation; he was assuring my privacy by entertaining the night watchman. I dropped into the dinghy, and pulled quietly across the river through the pink band of water that reflected the glare of London into the black band of water beneath the trees. My arrival was noticed only by a boy and girl, the inevitable boy and girl to be found in every dark corner of a great city. Better provision should be made for them – a Park of Temporary Affection, for example, from which lecherous clergymen and aged civil servants should be rigorously excluded. But such segregation is more easily accomplished by the uncivilized. Any competent witchdoctor could merely declare the Park taboo for all but the nubile.

It was nearly ten o'clock. I walked to the King's Road and found a grill-room where I ordered about all the meat they had to be put on the bars and served to me. While I waited I entered the telephone box to call my club. I always stay there when I have to be in London, and that I should stay there this time I never doubted until the door of the box shut behind me. Then I found that I could not telephone my club.

What excuses I gave myself at the moment, I can't remember. I think I told myself that it was too late, that they wouldn't have a room, that I didn't wish to walk through the vestibule in those clothes and in that condition.

After my supper, I took a bus to Cromwell Road and put up at one of those hotels designed for gentlewomen in moderately distressed circumstances. The porter didn't much care about taking me in, but fortunately I had a couple of pound notes and they had a room with a private bath; since their regular clientele could never afford such luxury, they were glad enough to let me the room. I gave them a false name and told them some absurd story to the effect that I had just arrived from abroad and had my luggage stolen. To digest my meal I read a sheaf of morning and evening papers, and then went to my room.

Their water, thank God, was hot! I had the most pleasurable bath that I ever remember. I have spent a large part of my life out of reach of hot baths; yet, when I enjoy a tub at leisure, I wonder why any man voluntarily deprives himself of so cheap and satisfying a delight. It rested and calmed me more than any sleep; indeed I had slept so much on the ship that my bath and my thoughts while lying in it had the flavour of morning rather than of night.

I understood why I had not telephoned my club. This was the first occasion on which I recognized that I had a second enemy dogging my movements – my own unjust and impossible conscience. Utterly unfair it was that I should judge myself as a potential murderer. I insist that I was always sure I could resist the temptation to press the trigger when my sights were actually on the target.

I have good reason now for a certain malaise. I have killed a man, though in self-defence. But then I had no reason at all. I may be wrong in talking of conscience; my trouble was, perhaps, merely a vision of the social effects of what I had done. This stalk of mine made it impossible for me to enter my club. How could I, for example, talk to Holy George after all the trouble I had caused him? And how could I expose my fellow members to the unpleasantness of being watched and perhaps questioned? No, I was an outlaw not because of my conscience (which, I maintain, has no right to torment me) but on the plain facts.

There was no lack of mirrors in the bathroom, and I made a thorough examination of my body. My legs and backside were an ugly mess – I shall carry some extraordinary scars for life – but the wounds had healed, and there was nothing any doctor could do to help. My fingers still appeared to have been squashed in a railway carriage door and then sharpened with a pen-knife, but they were in fact serviceable for all but very rough or very sensitive work. The eye was the only part of me that needed attention. I didn't propose to have anyone monkeying with it – I dared not give up any freedom of movement for the sake of regular treatment or an operation – but I wanted a medical opinion and whatever lotions would do it the most good.

In the morning I changed all the foreign money in my possession, and bought myself a passable suit off the peg. Then I got a list of eye specialists and taxied round and about Harley Street until I found a man who would see me at once. He was annoyingly inquisitive. I told him that I had hurt the eye at the beginning of a long voyage and had been out of reach of medical care ever since. When he had fully opened the lid, he fumed over my neglect, folly, and idiocy and declared that the eye had been burned as well as bruised. I agreed politely that it had and shut up; whereupon he became a doctor instead of a moralist and got down to business. He was honest enough to say that he could do nothing, that I'd be lucky if I ever perceived more than light and darkness, and that, on the whole, he recommended changing the real for a glass eye for the sake of appearance. He was wrong. My eye isn't pretty, but it functions better every day.

He wouldn't hear of my going about in dark glasses with no bandage, so I had him extend the bandages over the whole of my head. He humoured me in this, evidently thinking that I might get violent if opposed; my object was to give the impression of a man who had smashed his head rather than a man with a damaged eye. He was convinced that my face was familiar to him, and I allowed him to decide that we had once met in Vienna.

The next job was to see my solicitors in Lincoln's Inn Fields. The partner who has the entire handling of my estate is a man of about my own age and an intimate friend. He disapproves of me on only two grounds: that I refuse to sit on the board of any blasted company, and that I insist upon my right to waste money in agriculture. He doesn't mind my spending it on anything else, finding a vicarious pleasure in my travels and outlandish hobbies. He himself has a longing for a less ordered life, shown chiefly in his attitude to clothes. During the day he is sombrely and richly attired, and has even taken in recent years to wearing a black silk stock. At night he puts on tweeds, a sweater, and a tie that would frighten a newspaperman. One can't make him change for dinner. He would rather refuse an invitation.

Saul greeted me with concern rather than surprise; it was as if he had expected me to turn up in a hurry and the worse for wear. He locked the door and told his office manager we were not to be disturbed.

I assured him that I was all right and that the bandage was four times as long as was necessary. I asked what he knew and who had enquired for me.

He said that there had been a pointedly casual enquiry from Holy George, and that a few days later a fellow had come in to consult him about some inconceivable tangle under the Married Women's Property Act.

'He was so perfectly the retired military man from the West of England,' said Saul, 'that I felt he couldn't be real. He claimed to be a friend and neighbour of yours and was continually referring to you. When I cross-examined him a bit, it looked as if he had mugged up his case out of a law book and was really after information. Major Quive-Smith, he called himself. Ever heard of him?'

'Never,' I replied. 'He certainly isn't a neighbour of mine. Was he English?'

'I thought so. Did you expect him not to be English?'

I said I wasn't answering any of his innocent questions, that he was, after all, an Officer of the Court, and that I didn't wish to involve him.

'Tell me this much,' he said. 'Have you been abroad in the employ of our government?'

'No, on my own business. But I have to disappear.'

'You shouldn't think of the police as tactless,' he reminded me gently. 'A man in your position is protected without question. You've been abroad so much that I don't think you have ever realized the power of your name. You're automatically trusted, you see.'

I told him that I knew as much of my own people as he did – perhaps more, since I had been an exile long enough to see them from the outside. But I had to vanish. There was a risk that I might be disgraced.

A nasty word, that. I am not disgraced, and I will not feel it.

'Can I vanish? Financially, I mean?' I asked him. 'You have my power of attorney and you know more of my affairs than I do myself. Can you go on handling my estate if I am never heard of again?'

'So long as I know you are alive.'

'What do you mean by that?'

'A postcard this time next year will do.'

'X marks my window, and this is a palm tree?'

'Quite sufficient if in your own handwriting. You needn't even sign it.'

'Mightn't you be asked for proof?' I enquired.

'No. If I say you are alive, why the devil should it ever be questioned? But don't leave me without a postcard from time to time. You mustn't put me in the position of maintaining what might be a lie.'

I told him that if he ever got one postcard, he'd probably get a lot more; it was my ever living to write the first that was doubtful.

He blew up and told me I was absurd. He mingled abuse with affection in a way I hadn't heard since my father died. I didn't think he would take my disappearance so hard; I suppose he is as fond of me, after all, as I am of him, and that's saying a lot. He begged me again to let him talk to the police. I had no idea, he insisted, of the number and the subtle beauty of the strings that could be pulled.

I could only say I was awfully sorry, and after a silence I told him I wanted five thousand pounds in cash.

He produced my deed box and accounts. I had a balance of three thousand at the bank; he wrote his own cheque for the other two. That was like him – no nonsense about waiting for sales of stock or arranging an overdraft.

'Shall we go out and lunch while the boy is at the Bank?' he suggested.

'I think I'll leave here only once,' I said.

'You might be watched? Well, we'll soon settle that.'

He sent for Peale, a grey little man in a grey little suit whom I had only seen emptying the waste-paper baskets or fetching cups of tea.

'Anybody taking an interest in us, Peale?'

'There is a person in the gardens between Remnant Street and here feeding the birds. He is not very successful with them, sir' – Peale permitted himself a dry chuckle – 'in spite of the fact that he has been there for the past week during office hours. And I understand from Pruce & Fothergill that there are two other persons in Newman's Row. One of them is waiting for a lady to come out of their offices – a matrimonial case, I believe. The other is not known to us, and was observed to be in communication with the pigeon-man, sir, as soon as this gentleman emerged from his taxi.'

Saul thanked him, and sent him out to fetch us some beer and a cold bird.

I asked where he watched from, having a vague picture of Peale hanging over the parapet of the roof when he had nothing better to do.

'Good God, he doesn't watch!' exclaimed Saul, as if I had suggested a major impropriety. 'He just knows all the private detectives who are likely to be hanging around Lincoln's Inn Fields – on very good terms with them, I believe. They have to have a drink occasionally, and then they ask Peale or his counterpart in some other firm to keep his eyes open. When they see anyone who is not a member of the Trades Union, so to speak, they all know it.'

Peale came back with the lunch, and a packet of information straight from the counter of the saloon bar. The bird-man had been showing great interest in our windows and had twice telephoned. The chap in Newman's Row had hailed my taxi as it drove away. He would be able to trace me back to Harley Street and to the clothes shop, where, by a little adroit questioning, he could make an excuse to see the suit I discarded; my identification would be complete. It didn't much matter, since the watchers already had a strong suspicion that I was their man.

Peale couldn't tell us whether another watcher had been posted in Newman's Row or whether the other exits from Lincoln's Inn Fields were watched. I was certain that they were, and complained to Saul that all respectable firms of solicitors (who deal with far more scabrous affairs than the crooked) should have a back door. He replied that they weren't such fools as they looked, and that Peale could take me into Lincoln's Inn or the Law Courts and lose me completely.

Perhaps I should have trusted them; but I felt that, while their tricks might be good enough to lose a single private detective, I shouldn't be allowed to escape so easily. I decided to throw off the hunt in my own way.

When I kept my gloves on to eat, Saul forgot his official discretion and became an anxious friend. I think he suspected what had happened to me, though not why it had happened. I had to beg him to leave the whole subject alone.

After lunch, I signed a number of documents to tidy up loose ends, and we blocked out a plan I had often discussed with him of forming a sort of Tenants' Co-operative Society. Since I never make a penny out of the land, I thought they might as well pay rent to themselves, do their own repairs, and advance their own loans, with the right to purchase their own land by instalments at a price fixed by the committee. I hope it works. At any rate Saul and my land agent will keep them from quarrelling among themselves. I have no other dependants.

Then I told him something of the fisherman, and passed on the address that he had given me; we arranged for an income to be paid where it would do the most good – a discreet trust that couldn't conceivably be traced to me. It appeared to come from the estate of a recently defunct old lady who had left the bulk of her money to an institution for inoculating parrots against psittacosis, and the rest to any charitable object that Saul, as sole trustee, might direct.

There was nothing further to be done but arrange my cash in a body belt, and say good-bye. I asked him, if at any time a coroner sat on my body and brought in a verdict of suicide, not to believe it, but to make no attempt to reopen the case.

Peale walked with me across the square and into Kingsway by Gate Street. I observed that we were followed by a tall, inoffensive fellow in a dirty mackintosh and shabby felt hat, who was the bird-man. He looked the part. We also caught sight of a cheerful military man in Remnant Street, wearing a coat cut for riding and trousers narrower than were fashionable, whom Peale at once recognized as Major Quive-Smith. So I knew two at least whom I must throw off my track.

We parted at Holborn underground station, and I took a shilling ticket with which I could travel to the remotest end of London. The bird-man had got ahead of me. I passed him on the level of the Central London, and went down the escalator to the west-bound Piccadilly Tube. Ten seconds after I reached the platform, Major Quive-Smith also appeared upon it. He was gazing at the advertisements and grinning at the comic ones, as if he hadn't been in London for a year.

I pretended I had forgotten something, and shot out of the exit, up the stairs and down a corridor to the north-bound platform. No train was in. Even if there had been a train, the Major was too close behind for me to catch it and leave him standing.

I noticed that the shuttle train at the Aldwych left from the opposite side of the same platform. This offered a way of escape if ever there were two trains in at the same time.

The escalator took me back to the Central London level. The bird-man was talking to the chap in a glass-box at the junction of all the runways. I'd call him a ticket-collector but he never seems to collect any tickets; probably he is there to answer silly questions such as the bird-man was busily engaged in asking. I took the second escalator to the surface, and promptly dashed down again.

The bird-man followed me, but a bit late. We passed each other about midway, he going up and I going down and both running like hell. I thought I had him, that I could reach a Central London train before he could; but he was taking no risks. He vaulted over the division on to the stationary staircase. We reached the bottom separated only by the extra speed of my moving staircase – and that was a mere ten yards. The man in the glassbox came to life and said: ' 'Ere! You can't do that, you know!' But that didn't worry the bird-man. He was content to remain and discuss his anti-social action with the ticket-non-collector. I had already turned to the right into the Piccadilly Line and on to Major Quive-Smith's preserves.

At the bottom of the Piccadilly escalator you turn left for the north-bound trains, and continue straight on for the west-bound. To the right is the exit, along which an old lady with two side parcels was perversely trying to force her way against the stream of outcoming passengers. Major Quive-Smith was away to the left, at the mouth of the passage to the north-bound trains; so I plunged into the stream after the old lady, and was clear of it long before he was.

I ran on to the north-bound platform. An Aldwych shuttle was just pulling in, but there was no Piccadilly train. I shot under the Aldwych line, down to the west-bound platform, into the general exit, jamming him in another stream of outcoming passengers, and back to the north-bound Picca-dilly. There was a train standing, and the Aldwych shuttle had not left. I jumped into the Piccadilly train with the Major so far behind that he was compelled to enter another coach just as the doors were closing and just as I stepped out again.

Having thus despatched the Major to an unknown destination, I got into the Aldwych shuttle, which at once left on its half-mile journey.

This was all done at such a pace that I hadn't had time to think. I ought to have crossed to the west-bound Piccadilly and taken a train into the blue. But, naturally enough, I wanted to leave Holborn station as rapidly as possible, for fear of running into the bird-man or another unknown watcher if I waited. After half a minute in the Aldwych shuttle I realized that I had panicked like a rabbit in a warren. The mere couple of ferrets who had been after me had been magnified by my escape mechanism – a literal escape mechanism this, and working much faster than my mind – into an infinity of ferrets.

When we arrived at the Aldwych station and I was strolling to the lifts, I saw that it was not yet too late to return to Holborn. The bird-man would still be on the Central London level, for he might lose me if he left it for a moment. Quive-Smith couldn't have had time to telephone to anyone what had happened.

I turned back and re-entered the shuttle. The passengers were already seated in the single coach, and the platform clear; but a man in a black hat and blue flannel suit got in after me. That meant that he had turned back when I had turned back.

At Holborn I remained seated to prove whether my suspicions were correct. They were. Black Hat got out, sauntered around the platform, and got in again just before the doors closed. They had been far too clever for me! They had evidently ordered Black Hat to travel back and forth between Holborn and the Aldwych, and to go on travelling until either I entered that cursed coach or they gave him the signal that I had left by some other route. All I had done was to send Quive-Smith to Bloomsbury, whence no doubt he had already taken a taxi to some central clearing-point to which all news of my movements was telephoned.

As we left again for Aldwych, Black Hat was at the back of the coach and I was in the front. We sat as far away as possible from each other. Though we were both potential murderers, we felt, I suppose, mutual embarrassment. Mutual. I wish to God he had sat opposite me, or shown himself in some way less human than I.

The Aldwych station is a dead end. A passenger cannot leave it except by the lift or the emergency spiral staircase. Nevertheless I thought I had a wild chance of getting away. When the doors of the train opened, I dashed on to and off the platform, round a corner to the left and up a few stairs; but instead of going ten yards farther, round to the right and so to the lift, I hopped into a little blank alley that I had noticed on my earlier walk.

There was no cover of any sort, but Black Hat did just what I hoped. He came haring up the corridor, pushing through the passengers with his eyes fixed straight ahead, and jumped for the emergency staircase. The ticket collector called him back. He shouted a question whether anyone had gone up the stairs. The ticket collector, in turn, asked was it likely. Black Hat then entered the lift, and in the time it took him to get there and to glance over the passengers I was out of my alley and back on the platform.

The train was still in, but if I could catch it, so could Black Hat. The corridor was short, though with two right-angled twists, and he couldn't be more than five seconds behind me. I jumped on to the line and took refuge in the tunnel. There wasn't any employee of the Underground to see me except the driver, and he was in his box at the front of the coach. The platform of course, was empty.

Beyond the Aldwych station there seemed to be some fifty yards of straight tube, and then a curve, its walls faintly visible in a gleam of grey light. Where the tunnel goes, or if it ends in an odd shaft after the curve, I didn't have time to find out.

Black Hat looked through the coach and saw that I wasn't in it. The train pulled out, and when its roar had died away there was absolute silence. I hadn't realized that Black Hat and I would be left alone a hundred feet under London. I lay flattened against the wall in the darkest section of the tunnel.

The working of the Aldwych station is very simple. Just before the shuttle is due, the lift comes down. The departing passengers get into the train; the arriving passengers get into the lift. When the lift goes up and the train leaves, Aldwych station is as deserted as an ancient mine. You can hear the drip of water and the beat of your heart.

I can still hear them, and the sound of steps and his scream and the hideous, because domestic, sound of sizzling. They echoed along that tunnel which leads Lord knows where. A queer place for a soul to find itself adrift.

It was self-defence. He had a flash-light and a pistol. I don't know if he meant to use it. Perhaps he was only as frightened of me as I was of him. I crawled right to his feet and sprang at him. By God, I want to die in the open! If ever I have land again, I swear I'll never kill a creature below ground.

I lifted the bandages from my head and put them in my pocket; that expanse of white below my hat attracted too much attention to me. Then I came out, crossed the platform into the corridor, and climbed a turn of the emergency stairs. As soon as the lift came down, I mingled with the departing passengers and waited for the train. When it came in, I went up in the lift with the new arrivals. I gave up my shilling ticket and received a surprised glance from the collector since the fare from Holborn was but a penny. The only alternative was to pretend I had lost my ticket and to pay; that would have meant still closer examination. I left the station free, unwatched, unhurried, and took a bus back to the respectable squares of Kensington. Who would look for a fugitive between the Cromwell and Fulham roads? I dined at leisure, and then went to a cinema to think.

In these days of visas and identification cards it is impossible to travel without leaving a trail that can, with patience, bribery, and access to public records, be picked up. In the happy years between 1925 and 1930 you could talk yourself over any western European frontier, so long as you looked respectable and explained your movements and business with a few details that could be checked; you could treat frontier police as men of decency and common sense: two virtues that they could then afford to indulge. But now unless a traveller has some organization – subversive or benevolent – to help him, frontiers are an efficient bar to those who find it inconvenient or impossible to show their papers; and even if a frontier be crossed without record, there isn't the remotest village where a man can live without justifying himself and his reasons for being himself. Thus Europe, for me, was a mere trap with a delayed action.

Where, then, could I go? I thought at once of a job on a ship, for there's a shortage of seamen in these days; but it wasn't worth visiting shipping offices with my hands in the state they were. Rule out a long voyage as a stowaway. Rule out a discreet passage on a cargo ship. I could easily have got such a passage, but only by revealing my identity and presence in England to some friend. That I wanted to avoid at all costs. Only Saul, Peale, Vaner, and the admirable secret service which was hunting me knew that I wasn't in Poland. None of them would talk.

There remained a voyage in a passenger vessel. I could certainly get on to the ship without showing my passport; I might be able to get off it. But passenger lists are open to inspection, and if my name appeared on one some blasted reporter would consider it news and save my hunters trouble. They would, any way, be watching the lists themselves.

Then I needed a false passport. In normal circumstances I have no doubt that Saul or my friends in the Foreign Office could have arranged some tactful documentation for me, but, as it was, I could not involve any of them. It was unthinkable, just as police protection was unthinkable. I could not risk embarrassing the officials of my country. If the extraordinary being at whose waistcoat I had looked through a telescopic sight were moved by his daemon or digestion to poison international relations more than they already were, a very pretty case could be built up against a government that helped me to escape.

As I sat back in that cheap cinema seat, with my eyes closed and with the meaningless noises and music forcing my mind from plan to plan, I saw that I could only disappear by not leaving England at all. I must bury myself in some farm or country pub until the search for me had slackened.

When the main feature, as I believe they call it, was at its most dramatic quarter of an hour and the lavatory was likely to be empty, I left my seat, bathed my eye with the lotion the doctor had given me, and put on my bandages again. Then I wandered westwards through the quiet squares which smelled of a London August night – that perfume of dust and heavy flowers, held down by trees into the warm, well-dug ravines between the houses.

I decided against sleeping at a hotel. My position was

becoming so complicated that it seemed wise to occupy neutral territory whence I could move according to circumstances. A hotel porter might compel me into some act or lie that was unnecessary. I took a bus to Wimbledon Common; I had never been there, but knew there was a golf course and some sort of cover where corpses were very frequently discovered – indications of a considerable stretch of country that was open to the public at night.

The Common turned out to be ideal. I spent the night in a grove of silver birch where the fine soil – silver, too, it seemed to me, but the cause was probably the half-moon – held the heat of the day. There is, for me, no better resting-place than the temperate forests of Europe. Can one reasonably speak of forest at half an hour from Piccadilly Circus? I think so. The trees and heath are there, and at night one sees no paper bags.

In the morning I brushed off the leaves and bought a paper in a hurry from the local tobacconist as if I were briskly on my way to the City. In my new and too smart clothes I looked the part. ALDWYCH MYSTERY was occupying half a column of the centre page. I retired to a seat on the Common before committing myself to further dealings with the public.

The body had been discovered almost as soon as I was clear of the station. Foul play, said the paper cautiously, was suspected. In other words, the police were wondering how a man who had fallen on his back across the live rail could have suffered a smashing blow in the solar plexus.

The deceased had been identified. He was a Mr Johns who lived in a furnished room in those barrack squares of furnished rooms between Millbank and Victoria Station. His age, his friends, his background were unknown (and, if he knew his job always would be), but the paper carried an interview with his landlady. It must have been a horrible shock to be knocked up by a reporter around midnight and told that her lodger had been killed under suspicious circumstances. Or perhaps not. I have been assured by newspapermen that even close relatives forget their grief in the excitement of getting into the news; so a landlady, provided she had her rent, might not worry overmuch. Though knowing nothing whatever about the man under her roof, she had been most communicative. She said:

'He was a real gentlemen and I'm sure I don't know why anyone should have done him harm. His poor old mother will be broken-hearted.'

But it appeared that nobody had discovered the address of the poor old mother. The only evidence for her existence was the landlady's statement that she would often telephone Mr Johns, who thereupon rushed out in a great hurry to see her. I was not, of course, so cynical at the moment; but when the aged mother, such jam for journalists, was not mentioned at all in the evening papers, my conscience was easier.

The police were anxious to interview a well-dressed cleanshaven man in the early forties, with a bruised and blackened eye, who was observed to leave the Aldwych station shortly before the body was discovered, and surrendered a shilling ticket to the collector. I am not yet forty and I was not well dressed, but the description was accurate enough to be unpleasant reading.

It might have been worse. If they had wanted a man with a bandaged head, one of Saul's clerks might have let information leak, and the taxi-driver, who had, no doubt, already answered a number of mysterious questions, would have gone to the police. As it was, the public were left with the impression that the man's eye had been injured in the struggle below ground. No one except Saul and Mr Vaner could suspect that I might be the man concerned. Both of them would assume that the rights and wrongs were for my own conscience to settle rather than the police.

That confounded eye finished any chance I might have had of living in some obscure farm or inn. A wanted man with any well-marked peculiarity cannot hide in an English village. The local bobby has nothing to do but see that the pubs observe a decent discretion, if not the law, and that farmers do not too flagrantly ignore the mass of *paperasserie* that they are supposed to have read and haven't. He pushes his bicycle up the hills, dreaming of catching a real criminal, and when the usual chap with a scar or with a finger missing is wanted by the metropolitan police, every person of small means who has recently retired to a cottage (which puts him under suspicion anyway) is visited by the village bobby at unexpected times on the most improbable errands.

There was nothing for it but to live in the open. I sat on my bench on Wimbledon Common and considered what part of England to choose. The north was the wilder, but since I might have to endure a winter, the rigour of the climate was not inviting. My own county, though I carried the ordnance map in my eye and knew a dozen spots where I could go to ground, had to be avoided. I wonder what my tenants made of the gentleman who, at that time, was doubtless staying at the Red Lion, asking questions, and describing himself as a hiker who had fallen in love with the village. A hideous word – hiker. It has nothing to do with the gentle souls of my youth who wandered in tweeds and stout shoes from pub to pub. But, by God, it fits those bawling English-women whose tight shorts and loose voices are turning every beauty spot in Europe into a Skegness holiday camp.

I chose southern England, with a strong preference for Dorset. It is a remote county, lying as it does between

Hampshire, which is becoming an outer suburb, and Devon which is a playground. I knew one part of the county very well indeed, and, better still, there was no reason for anyone to suppose that I knew it. I had never hunted with the Cattistock. I had no intimate friends nearer than Somerset. The business that had taken me to Dorset was so precious that I kept it to myself.

There are times when I am no more self-conscious than a chimpanzee. I had chosen my destination to within ten yards; yet, that day, I couldn't have told even Saul where I was going. This habit of thinking about myself and my motives has grown upon me only recently. In this confession I have forced myself to analyse; when I write that I did this because of that, it is true. At the time of the action, however, it was not always true; my reasons were insistent but frequently obscure.

Though the precise spot where I was going was no more nor less present in my consciousness than the dark shadows which floated before my left eye, I knew I had to have a fleece-lined, waterproof sleeping-bag. I dared not return to the centre of London, so I decided to telephone and have the thing sent COD to Wimbledon station by a commissionaire.

I spoke to the shop in what I believed to be a fine disguised bass voice, but the senior partner recognized me almost at once. Either I gave myself away by showing too much knowledge of his stock, or my sentence rhythm is unmistakable.

'Another trip, sir, I suppose?'

I could imagine him rubbing his hands with satisfaction at my continued custom.

He mentioned my name six times in one minute of ejaculations. He burbled like a fatherly butler receiving the prodigal son.

I had to think quickly. To deny my identity would evidently cause a greater mystery than to admit it. I felt pretty safe with him. He was one of the few dozen blackcoated archbishop-like tradesmen of the West End – tailors, gunsmiths, bootmakers, hatters – who would die of shame rather than betray the confidence of a customer, to whom neither the law nor the certainty of a bad debt is as anything compared to the pride of serving the aristocracy.

'Can anyone hear you?' I asked him.

I thought he was probably chucking my name about for the benefit of a shop assistant or a customer. These ecclesiasts of Savile Row and Jermyn Street are about the only true dyed-in-the-wool snobs that are left.

He hesitated an instant. I imagined him looking round. I knew the telephone was in the office at the far end of the shop.

'No, sir,' he said with a shade of regret that made me certain he was telling the truth.

I explained to him that I wished no one to know I was in England and that I trusted him to keep my name off his lips and out of his books. He oozed dutifulness – and thoughtfulness too, for after much humming and hawing and excusing himself he asked me if I would like him to bring me some cash together with the sleeping-bag. I very possibly had not wished to visit my bank, he said. Wonderful fellow! He assumed without any misgiving at all that his discretion was greater than that of my bank manager. I wouldn't be surprised if it was.

Since I was in for it anyway, I gave him a full list of my requirements – a boy's catapult, a billhook, and the best knife he had; toilet requisites and a rubber basin; a Primus stove and a pan; flannel shirts, heavy trousers and underclothes, and a wind-proof jacket. Within an hour he was at

Wimbledon station in person, with the whole lot neatly strapped into the sleeping-bag. I should have liked a firearm of some sort, but it was laying unfair weight on his discretion to ask him not to register or report the sale.

I took a train to Guildford, and thence by slow stages to Dorchester, where I arrived about five in the afternoon. I changed after Salisbury, where a friendly porter heaved my roll into an empty carriage on a stopping train without any corridor. By the time we reached the next station I was no longer the well-dressed man. I had become a holiday-maker with Mr Vaner's very large and dark sun-glasses.

I left my kit at Dorchester station. What transport to take into the green depths of Dorset I hadn't the faintest notion. I couldn't buy a motor vehicle or a horse because of the difficulty of getting rid of them. A derelict car or a wandering horse at once arouses any amount of enquiry. To walk with my unwieldy roll was nearly impossible. To take a bus merely puts off the moment when I would have to find more private conveyance.

Strolling as far as the Roman amphitheatre, I lay on the outer grass slope to watch the traffic on the Weymouth road and hope for an idea. The troops of cyclists interested me. I hadn't ridden a cycle since I was a boy, and had forgotten its possibilities. These holiday-makers carried enough gear on their backs and mudguards to last a week or two, but I didn't see how I could balance my own camping outfit on a bike.

I waited for an hour, and along came the very vehicle I wanted. I have since noticed that they are quite common on the roads, but this was the first I had seen. A tandem bicycle it was, with pa and ma riding and the baby slung alongside in a little side-car. I should never have dared to carry any offspring of mine in a contraption like that, but I must admit that for a young couple with no nerves and little money it was a sensible way of taking a holiday.

I stood up and yelled to them, pointing frantically at nothing in particular. They dismounted, looked at me with surprise, then at baby, then at the back-wheel.

'Sorry to stop you,' I said. 'But might I ask you where you bought that thing? Just what I want for me and the missus and the young 'un!'

I thought that struck the right note.

'I made it,' said pa proudly.

He was a boy of about twenty-three or -four. He had the perfect self-possession and merry eyes of a craftsman. One can usually spot them, this new generation of craftsmen. They know the world is theirs, and are equally contemptuous of the professed radical and the genteel. They definitely belong in Class X, though I suppose they must learn to speak the part before being recognized by so conservative a nation.

'Are you in the cycle trade?'

'Not me!' he answered with marked scorn for his present method of transport. 'Aircraft!'

I should have guessed it. The aluminium plating and the curved, beautifully tooled ribs had the professional touch; and two projections at the front of the side-car, which at first glance I had taken for lamps, were obviously model machine-guns. I hope they were for pa's amusement rather than for the infant's.

'He looks pretty comfortable,' I said to the wife.

She was a sturdy wench in corduroy shorts no longer than bum-bags, and with legs so red that the golden hairs showed as continuous fur. Not my taste at all. But my taste is far from eugenic.

' 'E loves it, don't you, duck?'

She drew him from the side-car as if uncorking a fat puppy from a riding-boot. I take it that she did not get hold of him by the scruff of the neck, but my memory insists that she did. The baby chortled with joy, and made a grab for my dark glasses.

'Now, Rodney, leave the poor gentleman alone!' said his mother.

That was fine. There was a note of Pity the Blind about her voice. Mr Vaner's glasses had no delicate tints. They turned the world dark blue.

'You wouldn't like to sell it, I suppose?' I asked, handing pa a cigarette.

'I might when we get home,' he answered cautiously. 'But my home's Leicester.'

I said I was ready to make him an offer for bicycle and side-car then and there.

'And give up my holiday?' he laughed. 'Not likely, mister!'

'Well, what would it cost?'

'I wouldn't let it go a penny under fifteen quid!'

'I might go to twelve pounds ten,' I offered – I'd have gladly offered him fifty for it, but I had to avoid suspicion. 'I expect I could buy the whole thing new for that, but I like your side-car and the way it's fixed. My wife is a bit nervous, you see, and she'd never put the nipper in anything that didn't look strong.'

'It is strong,' he said. 'And fifteen quid would be my last word. But I can't sell it you, because what would we do?'

He hesitated and seemed to be summing up me and the bargain. A fine, quick-witted mind he had. Most people would be far too conservative to consider changing a holiday in the middle.

'Haven't anything you'd like to swap?' he asked. 'An old car or rooms at the seaside? We'd like a bit of beach to sit on,

but what with doctor's bills and the missus so extrava-
gant . . .'

He gave me a broad wink, but the missus wasn't to be
drawn.

'He's one for kidding!' she informed me happily.

'I've got a beach hut near Weymouth,' I said. 'I'll let you
have it free for a fortnight, and ten quid for the combination.'

The missus gave a squeal of joy, and was sternly frowned
upon by her husband.

'I don't know as I want a beach hut,' he said, 'and it would
be twelve quid. Now we're going to Weymouth tonight. Now
suppose we did a swap, could we move in right away?'

I told him he certainly could, so long as I could get there
ahead of him to fix things up and have the place ready. I said
I would see if there were a train.

'Oh, ask for a lift!' he said, as if it were the obvious way of
travelling any short distance. 'I'll soon get you one.'

That chap must have had some private countersign to the
freemasonry of the road. Myself, I never have the impudence
to stop a car on a main road. Why, I don't know. I'm always
perfectly willing to give a lift if I am driving.

He let half a dozen cars go by, remarking 'toffs!', and then
stopped one unerringly. It was a battered Morris, very much
occupied by a sporty-looking gent who might have been a
bookmaker or a publican. He turned out to be an employee
of the County Council whose job it was to inspect the steam-
rollers.

'Hey, mister! Can you give my pal a lift to Weymouth?'

'Look sharp, then!' answered the driver cheerily.

I arranged to meet the family at the station at seven-thirty,
and got in.

He did the eight miles to Weymouth in a quarter of an
hour. I explained that I was hopping on ahead to get rooms

for the rest of our cycling party when they arrived, and asked him if he knew of any beach huts for rent. He said there weren't any beach huts, and that, what was more, we should find it difficult to get rooms.

'A wonderful season!' he said. 'Sleeping on the beach they were at Bank Holiday!'

This was depressing. I had evidently been rash in my offer for the family combination. I told him that I personally intended to stay some time in Weymouth, and what about a tent or a bungalow or even one of those caravans the steam-roller men slept in?

That amused him like anything.

'Ho!' he said. 'They're county property, they are! They wouldn't let you have one of them things. But I tell you what!' – he lowered his voice confidentially in the manner of the English when they are proposing a deal (it comes, I think, from the national habit of buying and selling in a public bar) – 'I know a trailer you could buy cheap, if you were thinking of buying, that is.'

He drove me to a garage kept by some in-law of his, where there was a whacking great trailer standing in the yard amid a heap of scrap-iron. It appeared home-made by some enthusiast who had forgotten, in his passion for roominess and gadgets, that it had to be towed round corners behind a car. The in-law and the steam-roller man showed me over that trailer as if they were a couple of high-powered estate agents selling a mansion. It was a little home from home, they said. And it was! It had everything for two except the bedding, and it was mine for forty quid. I accepted their price on condition that they threw in the bedding and a cot for Rodney, and towed me then and there to a camp-site. They drove me a couple of miles to the east of Weymouth where there was an open field with a dozen tents and trailers. I rented a site for six months from the landowner and told him that friends would be occupying the trailer for the moment, and that I myself hoped to get down for many weekends in the autumn. He showed no curiosity whatever; if strange beings chose to camp on his land he collected five bob a week from them in advance and never went near them again.

When we got back to the town, I had a quick drink with my saviours and vanished. It was nearly eight before I could reach the station. Pa and ma were leaning disconsolately against the railings.

'Now then, mister,' said my aircraft mechanic, 'time's money, and how about it?'

He was a little peeved at my being late. Evidently he had been thinking the luck too good to be true, and that he wouldn't see me again.

We walked wearily out to the camp-site. The trailer was quite enchanting in the gathering dusk, and I damn near gave it to them. Well, at any rate he got his fortnight's holiday rent-free, and I expect he managed to replace tandem and side-car for the twelve quid. I said that I should probably be back before the end of his fortnight, but that, if I was not, he should give the key to the landowner. I don't think the trailer can be the object of any enquiry until the six months are up; and by that time I hope to be out of England.

I rode the beastly combination back to Weymouth, spilling myself into the ditch at the first left-hand corner, for it wasn't easy to get the hang of it. Then I had a meal and, finding that the snack-bars and tea-shops were still open, filled up the side-car with a stock of biscuits and a ham, plenty of tinned foods and fruits, tobacco, and a few bottles of beer and whisky. At the third shop I entered, a dry-faced spinster gazed into my glasses long and suspiciously, and remarked:

"Urt your eye, 'ave you?"

I answered unctuously that it was an infliction from birth, and that I feared it was the Lord's will to take from me the sight of the other eye. She became most sympathetic after that, but I had had my warning.

I cycled through the darkness to Dorchester, arriving there dead-beat about midnight. I picked up my kit and strapped it on the side-car. Then I pedalled a few miles north into the silence of a valley where the only moving thing was the Frome gurgling and gleaming over the pebbles. I wheeled my combination off the road and into a copse, unpacked, and slept.

The bag was delicious. In a month I had only spent half a night in bed. I slept and slept, brought up to consciousness at intervals by the stirring of leaves or insects, but seizing upon sleep again as effortlessly as pulling a blanket over one's ears.

It was after ten when I awoke. I lay in my fleece till noon, looking up through the oak leaves to a windy sky and trying to decide whether it were less risky to travel by day or night. If by day, I should arouse no particular curiosity, but my vehicle was so odd that dozens of people would remember having seen it; if by night, anyone who saw me would talk about me for days. But between midnight and three nothing stirs in farm or village. I was prepared to gamble that nobody would see me.

I admitted to myself now where I was going. The road I meant to take was a narrow track along the downs, a remnant of the old Roman road from Dorchester to Exeter, only used by farmers' carts. My meeting with any human being in the darkness was most improbable. Even if I were not alone on the hills, I should hear before I was heard. I remembered how in that wheat-field I had cursed the silent approach of cyclists.

My temporary camp was fairly safe, though close to a road. All day I saw no one but a most human billy-goat belonging to a herd of cows in the neighbouring field. He had a look at the side-car and ate some twigs of the bush under which it was resting. He spat them out again, regarding me ironically. He reminded me of some old whiskered countryman solemnly walking over a right-of-way which isn't the slightest use to him, in order to keep it open. I like to see a billy-goat accompanying the dairy herd to pasture, supposedly to bring them luck or to eat the herbs that cause abortion. I think his true function has been forgotten, but there is no object in going against ancient tradition, nor reason to suppose he has no function.

I started at midnight. The first three miles were on a well-used by-road, but I met only one car. I had time to lean my bicycle against a hedge and to get over into the field myself. The Roman road was teeming with life: sheep and cows lying on it, rabbits dancing in and out of ancient pits, owls gliding and hooting over the thorn. I carried no light, and was continually upsetting in the ruts, for the space between them was only just wide enough to take my three wheels. Eventually I dismounted and walked.

What with the slow going and losing my way in a maze of tracks and gorse-bushes, the hedges were beginning to take shape in the half-light when I coasted down into the vale, crossed the railway, and slipped silently through the sleeping village of Powerstock. It was time to leave the road. In the neighbouring fields, so far as I could search them with one eye – and that still unused to judging perspective – there was little cover. When I came upon the four walls of a burned and derelict cottage, I laid the tandem in the nettles that covered the old floor and detached the side-car, which I half hid under bricks and debris. I made no attempt to conceal myself, lying down in the long grass beside a stream. It was a warm, silent day, beginning with a September mist that hung low over the meadows. If anyone saw me, I was really sleeping or pretending to sleep with my head on my arms – a common enough sight by any stream in holiday time.

I reassembled my vehicle in the dusk, and started at eleven. There were no villages, and the only checks were at the crossing of two main roads. The dogs barked and cursed at me as I passed solitary farms and cottages, but I was out of sight before the householders could look out of their windows, if they ever did. I rode swiftly, for there was much to be done that night.

At half-past twelve I was on the ridge of a half-moon of low rabbit-cropped hills, the horns of which rested upon the sea, enclosing between them a small, lush valley. The outer or northern slopes look down upon the Marshwood Vale. Here I passed out of the chalk into the sandstone; the lanes, worn down by the packhorses of a hundred generations plodding up from the sea on to the dry, hard going of the ridges, were fifteen feet or more below the level of the fields. These trade-worn cantons of red and green upon the flanks of the hills are very dear to me.

I pushed my combination along the ridge until I came to a lane that dived down into the valley. In the dark I could hardly recognize it. I remembered it as a path, deep indeed, but dappled with sunlight; it looked to me now a cleft eroded in desert country, for its bottom was only a cart's width across, and its sides, with the banks, the hedges above them and young oaks leaping up from the hedge, seemed fifty feet of solid blackness.

I followed it down until another lane crossed at a right angle; this led northwards back to the ridge, where it came up to the surface and branched into two farm tracks. These two tracks appear to be the end and aim of the ancient little high-road, but if you ignore them and walk across an acre of pasture you come to a thick hedge running downhill into the Marshwood Vale. In the heart of this hedge, which I had been seeking all the way from London, the lane reappears. It is not marked on the map. It has not been used, I imagine, for a hundred years.

The deep sandstone cutting, its hedges grown together across the top, is still there; anyone who wishes can dive under the sentinel thorns at the entrance and push his way through and come out in a cross hedge that runs along the foot of the hills. But who would wish? Where there is light, the nettles grow as high as a man's shoulder; where there is not, the lane is choked by dead wood. The interior of the double hedge is of no conceivable use to the two farmers whose boundary fence it is, and nobody but an adventurous child would want to explore it.

That, indeed, was the manner of its finding. In love one becomes a child again. A rock is a cliff, a hedge a forest, a stream a river flowing to God knows what Arcadies. This lane was our discovery, a perilous passage made for us to force. It was only the spring of this year that I took her to England, choosing the Dorset downs to give her the first sight and feeling of the land that was to be her home. It was her last sight, too. I cannot say that we had any sense of premonition, unless the tenseness of our love. There is a desperate sweetness between man and woman when the wings of the four horsemen drone inwards from the corners of their world.

It was now my job to prevent children or lovers pushing through that way again. I worked the side-car into the thicket and deposited it in the first bare stretch of lane, where the foliage overhead was so thick that nothing grew but ferns.

Then I unpacked the bill-hook and slashed at the dead wood on the inside of the hedges. I jammed the bicycle cross-wise between the banks and piled over it a hedge of thorn that would have stopped a lion. At the lower end of the lane the trailing brambles were sufficient defence, and I reinforced them with a dead holly-bush. That was all I dared do for the moment. The light was growing, and the strokes of my hook echoing down the hillside.

I cut steps up the western bank and up the inner side of a young elm; it had a top-heavy branch hanging low over the hedge and within reach of the ground on the farther side. This elm became my way in and out of the lane. I spent most of the day up the tree, whence I had a clear view to the north and west. I wanted to watch the routine of the neighbouring farms and to see if I had overlooked any danger.

The field on the east of the lane was rough pasture. An hour after dawn the cows came wandering into it over the skyline, having been driven through a gate which I could not see. Farther to the east was a down where the short turf was only good for sheep. To the west, immediately below my tree, was a forty-acre field of wheat stubble, falling away sharply to a great, grey, prosperous farm with generous barns and a duck-pond.

It was as quiet a hillside as any in England. The activities of the farm below me were chiefly in the vale. Of the inhabitants of the farm to the east I saw none, only heard the boy who called the cows home in the evening – which he did without ever entering the pasture. In the lanes of the Marshwood Vale there was little traffic. I saw the postman with his motor-bike and red side-car. I saw the schoolbus and an occasional car, and a couple of milk lorries bobbing about among the trees to collect the cans set out on wooden platforms by the road or on the pebble bottoms of the streams.

The section of lane that I had chosen was so damp and dark that the roots which crept over the earth were white. In the evening I moved my possessions farther down into a tiny glade of bracken where the sun shone for three hours a day. It was protected by the high banks, topped by untrimmed hedges of ash, and buttressed on the east by bushes of blackberry and sloe extending far out into the pasture.

I cut the bracken and scraped out a channel for the stream that ran down the lane after every shower. Then I slung ash-poles from bank to bank – where the distance was a bare six feet – making a monkey's platform on top of them with twigs and bracken. A day or two later, when I stole some bricks from a tumbledown barn and propped up my poles in the middle, the platform was as strong and dry as a floor of laths.

The eastern bank was full of rabbit holes which ran into the heavy topsoil along the upper level of the sandstone. On this same night I began the work on them which has provided me with shelter from the rain and with a hearth. By morning I had made a hollow about two feet in diameter and long enough to receive my body. The roof and sides were of earth and the floor of sandstone.

Burrowing into the stone, soft though it was, proved an interminable job; but I found that it was easy to scrape away the surface, and thus lower the floor inch by inch. In a week I had a shelter to be proud of. The roof had a high vault, packed with clay. The drip trickled down the sides and was caught on two projecting ledges which ran the length of the burrow and were channelled to lead the water into the lane. The floor was three feet below the level of the ledges and crossed by short faggots of ash which kept my sleeping-bag from resting on damp stone. The hole was very much the size and shape of two large bath-tubs, one inverted upon the other.

As soon as my beard had grown, I walked to Beaminster and came back with knapsack full of groceries, a grill, iron spits, and a short pick, one arm of which was shaped like a miniature battle-axe. I do not know what it is for, but it seemed admirably fitted for working sandstone in a confined space. I aroused no particular interest in Beaminster – a mere untidy holiday-maker with dark glasses – and gave out that I was camping on the hills just across the Somerset border. I had a meal in an inn and read the papers. There was only a passing reference to the Aldwych Mystery. The verdict had been murder by a person or persons unknown. When I climbed down the elm into the lane I felt that I had come home – a half-melancholy sense of slippered relaxation.

I began a routine of sleeping by day and working on the burrow at night. Working by day was too dangerous; someone might walk past the hedge while I was underground, and hear the noise of the pick. There was a morning when I was nearly caught by a party of children picking blackberries on the edge of the pasture.

I ran the hole a good ten feet back into the bank and then drove a gallery to the right, intending only to make a hearth; but I found the stone so split by tree-roots and easily worked that I ended the gallery with a bee-hive grotto in which I could comfortably squat. After some difficult surface measurements (by sticking a pole through the hedge and climbing out to see where the tip had got to) I drove a chimney straight upwards into the centre of a blackberry bush. I could then risk a fire at night and cook fresh food.

All this while I had wondered why it was that I had no trouble with dogs. I was so prepared to frighten any dogs which investigated me that they would never come back, but it appeared that something had already scared them for me; dogs gave the lane a wide berth. The cause was Asmodeus. I observed him first as two ears and two eyes apparently attached to a black branch. When I moved my head, the ears vanished, and when I stood up the rest of him had vanished. I put out some scraps of bully beef behind the branch, and an hour later they too had vanished.

One morning when I had just gone to bed, and was lying with my head out of the burrow chewing biscuits, he slunk on to my platform and watched me, tail gripping the ground, head savage and expectant. He was a thin and powerful tom-cat, black, but with many of his hairs ending in a streak of silver, like a smooth-headed Mediterranean beauty just turning grey. I don't think that in his case it is age, but a freak of colouring inherited from some silver ancestor. I threw him a biscuit; he was out of sight while it was still in the air. It had gone, of course, when I woke up, and so had half a tin of bully beef.

He began to consider me as a curious show for his leisure hours, sitting motionless at a safe distance of ten feet. In a few more days he would snatch food from my hand, hissing and bristling if I dared advance the hand to touch him. It was then that I named him Asmodeus for he could make himself appear the very spirit of hatred, and malignity.

I won his friendship with a pheasant's head, attached to the end of a string. I have noticed that what cats most appreciate in a human being is not the ability to produce food – which they take for granted – but his or her entertainment value. Asmodeus took to his toy enthusiastically. In another week he permitted me to stroke him, producing a raucous purr, but, in order to save his face, pretending to be asleep. Soon afterwards he started a habit of sleeping in the burrow with me during the day, and hunting while I worked at night. But bully beef was the meat he preferred; no doubt it gave him the maximum nourishment for the minimum effort.

I made two more journeys to Beaminster, walking there and back at night and spending the intervening day – after doing my shopping – hidden on a hillside of gorse. From the first expedition I returned with food and paraffin for the Primus; from the second with a glue-pot and a small door which I had ordered from the local carpenter.

This door or lid fitted exactly into the entrance to my burrow. On the inside was a stout handle by which I could lift and jam it into position; on the outside was camouflage. I sprinkled over a coating of glue a rough layer of sandstone dust, and on that stuck an arrangement of twigs and dead plants, some of which trailed over the edges of the door so that they masked the outline when it was in place.

As soon as I was satisfied with the door, I practised a drill for effacing myself completely from the lane. The platform was dismantled, the bricks were scattered, and the poles thrust into the hedge; my latrine and rubbish-pit were covered by a dead thorn, and I myself was inside in the burrow, all in ten minutes. Anyone forcing a way into the lane might or might not notice that some gypsy had been camping there, but could not guess that the place was inhabited at the moment. The only sign was an apparent rabbit-hole, a bit artificial in spite of the droppings I scattered round the entrance, which gave me air while I was shut in the burrow.

The tandem bicycle could not be seen. I took it apart and propped the pieces against the bank, covering them with a mass of dead vegetation. The side-car was a continual nuisance. I couldn't bury it or take it to bits, and the bright aluminium shone through the brushwood I heaped on it. It was so new and strong that no one could be deceived into thinking it innocently abandoned. Eventually I had to spend a night tearing down my defences in order to get the thing out of the lane, and half wheeling, half carrying it down to the vale.

I didn't know what on earth to do with it. Wherever I put it, it might be found, and the more remote the place, the more the question as to how it came there. Nor could I waste any time; if I met anyone, he would see my gleaming and awkward burden long before I saw him. Finally I chucked it into a sheltered stream, hoping that the action of water would destroy it; I couldn't.

I am now prepared to spend the first half of the winter where I am, subject to the bottom of the lane being still invisible when the leaves have fallen – which seems probable. I cannot be seen and, if I am careful, I cannot be heard. I avoid chopping wood and risk the noise of my bill-hook only on one night a week when I fill the inner chamber with brushwood and burn it. This dries out the whole den and gives me a layer of hot ashes on which I can grill at one time whatever store of meat I have.

My dry and tinned food is sufficient, for I have been living largely on the country. There are cob-nuts, sloes, and blackberries at my door, and from time to time I extract a bowl of milk from a red cow; she has a great liking for salt, and can be tempted to stand quietly among the domes and ramps of blackberry bush that flank the eastern hedge.

My catapult keeps me supplied with the rabbits I want. It's an inefficient weapon. As one whose hobby is the craft of ballistics, ancient and modern, I ought to be ashamed of myself for depending on rubber when a far better weapon could be made from twisted hair or cord. But I have a distaste for the whole business. I have to compel myself to shoot a rabbit in these days. After all, it is perfectly justifiable to kill for food.

I am not content, in spite of the fact that this Robinson

Crusoe existence ought to suit my temperament pretty well. There is not, any longer, enough to do. I am not affected by loneliness nor by the memories of this place. Asmodeus helps there. He is a ridiculous outlet for a lot of sentimentality. I am uncertain of myself. Even this journal, which I was sure would exorcise my misgivings, has settled nothing.

start on this exercise book again, for I dare not leave my thoughts uncontrolled. Sitting below the ventilator, I have just enough light. It is good to hold the white page before it. My eyes as well as my mind long for some object on which to concentrate.

A month ago I wrote that I did not feel lonely. It was true, and it accounts for my folly. The essence of safety is that a hunted man should feel lonely; then his whole being throws out tendrils, as it were, towards the outer world. He becomes swift to imagine, sensitive as an animal to danger. But I, I was sunk in a gentle, moody preoccupation with my cat and my conscience. Dear God, I might as well have been a retired company director living in a solitary cottage and mildly worried whether his speculations were discovered!

I committed the supreme folly of writing to Saul to send me books. Once my earth was finished, I had too much leisure and no use for it. Besides all my other incoherent dissatisfactions, questions of sex were worrying me.

For me, sex has never been a problem. Like most normal people, I have been able to suppress my desires without difficulty. When there was no need to suppress them, my appreciation has been keen, but my emotions have not been deeply involved. Indeed, I begin to think that I have never known truly passionate love. I have no doubt that, say, an Italian would consider me the perfect type of frigid Anglo-Saxon.

Why, then, my strong resistance to coming to this lane? I take it that I showed a resistance, since I refused to admit to myself that this was my destination until I was within twenty miles of it – and that though the double hedge was an excellent hiding-place which I was eager to reach. Well, I suppose I wished to save myself pain. But I cannot even remember her face, except that her eyes appeared violet against the tawny skin. And that I know to be a trick of memory, for I have often looked for violet eyes in man and woman and never seen them. I repeat, I was never in love. The proof of it is that I so calmly accepted the destruction of my happiness. I was prepared for it. I begged her to stay in England, or at least, if she felt it her duty to return, to temper her politics with discretion. When I heard that she was dead, I really suffered very little.

I wrote to Saul for books: meaty stuff which I could re-read throughout the winter, penetrating with each reading a little further into what the author meant rather than what he said. I did not, of course, sign the letter, but wrote in block capitals, asking him to send the books to Professor Foulsham at a sub-post office in Lyme Regis. Foulsham was (and still is, I trust) the professor of Christian Ethics in my day, and it seemed to me that my hairy face looked rather like his. It probably didn't; but it is always well to choose and think oneself into a part.

I did not wish to see Beaminster any more. While the holiday season was still on, my three visits and my account of myself naturally passed unchallenged, but a man who claimed to be still camping on the downs in the gathering gales of October would start any amount of gossip about where he was and why. I picked Lyme Regis because the little town had a winter colony of visitors and strangers presumably attracted no attention.

I had a straggly beard that was quite as convincing as most of those one sees in Bloomsbury. My eye, as a result of continual washing in dew and lotion, was no longer swollen; it looked odd, but more like a bad glass eye than a wounded one. There was nothing in my appearance of a harmless and rather dirty eccentric to arouse the curiosity of the police. As for my other enemies, they had then no more reason to search Dorset than Kamchatka.

I walked to the outskirts of the town in a couple of hours before dawn, and concealed myself during the day in the shrubbery of a large empty house. In the evening I called at the post office, introduced myself as Professor Foulsham, and asked if a parcel of books had come for me. It was one of those small, dark shops that sell stationery and tobacco, and have a back room with the inevitable pot of tea stewing by the fire.

'Sorry! There is no parcel in that name,' said the postmistress.

I asked if there were a letter.

'I think there may be,' she said archly, and reached under the counter for half a dozen letters.

A woman who had been examining a row of dress-making magazines hung on strings across the window said good night and opened the door, letting the last of the evening light into the shop. The postmistress stared at me as if her eyes had stuck – shoe-button eyes they were, sharp and nervous.

'There – there's more letters in the back room,' she stammered, and edged through the door into the parlour, still watching me.

I heard frantic whispering, and a girl's voice say: 'Oo, Ma, I couldn't do that!' – followed by a resounding slap.

A schoolgirl of about twelve dashed out of the back room, dived under the flap of the counter, and with one terrified glance at me bolted down the road. The postmistress remained at the threshold of her room, still fascinated by my appearance.

I didn't like the look of things, but what was wrong I couldn't imagine. I was wearing my reach-me-down suit and muffler, and had succeeded, I thought, in impersonating a weatherproof don on his hardy way from a tea-party. I left my glasses at home, believing that I should attract less attention without those tremendous blinkers. As a matter of fact it would have made no difference whether I wore them or not.

'Now, madam,' I said severely, 'if you can bring yourself to attend to public business, I should like my letter.'

'Don't you dare come near me!' she squeaked, shrinking back into the doorway.

It was no time for respecting His Majesty's mails. She had dropped the letters behind the wire enclosure which protected her cash and stamps. I reached over it, and took an envelope addressed to Professor Foulsham.

'Kindly satisfy yourself, madam,' I said, seeing that she was mustering courage to scream, 'that this letter is actually addressed to me. I regret that it will be my duty to report your extraordinary behaviour. Good afternoon.'

This pomposity, delivered in a most professorial tone, held her with her mouth open long enough for me to move with dignity out of the shop. I jumped on a bus that was running uphill out of the town, and got off it ten minutes later at a cross-roads on the Devon and Dorset border. Safe for the moment in the thick cover of a spinney I opened my letter, hoping it would tell me why a description of me had been circulated to Dorset post offices.

The letter was typewritten and unsigned, but Saul had made his identity certain. He wrote in some such words as these:

'The parrots paid the fisherman. I must not send you books in case they are found and traced to the buyer. If you know nothing of a caravan trailer, write to me again and I will risk it.

'About two weeks ago the police tried to find the owner of a trailer near Weymouth. It was a routine enquiry. The camp-site was deserted, and the landlord did not wish to be held responsible for damage done by children who had broken a window and were climbing in and out of the trailer.

'The police established that the owner had bought and let the caravan on the same evening, that this was the evening after a man had been found killed in the Aldwych station, and that the owner wore dark glasses.

'They then got in touch with a family at Leicester who had rented the thing. They learned that the owner had taken, in exchange for rent, a tandem bicycle and baby's side-car, and that he had told a lot of complicated untruths to account for himself.

'A woman in Weymouth from whom he bought food is sure that under his glasses one eye was worse than the other, but no one else noticed this.

'The man is wanted for murder, but if the case, as I think it must, depends solely on doubtful identification by a ticket-collector, no jury would convict. And let me very urgently impress it on you that if the man were a person of good character, if he pleaded self-defence and gave good reason for the attack made upon him, the case would never go to court. I earnestly advise this course. The dead man was a thoroughly undesirable fellow, suspected of being in the pay of a foreign power.

'The owner of the trailer is certain to be found and detained, for he is known to be camping or living in the open on the downs near Beaminster. A person who had grown a beard but otherwise answered his description was seen three times at Beaminster before any police enquiries had begun.

'I have naturally kept myself fully informed of the Aldwych investigation, and you can take it as certain that the police know as much as I have told you and no more.'

He ended with a request to me to burn the letter immediately, which I did.

I had little fear of my burrow being discovered, and my first reaction was to thank heaven that I now knew the worst and had been warned in time. But then I perceived the full extent of my folly, and its consequences; a desultory search which had spread over the whole of Dorset, and especially over the Dorset downs miles to the north-east of where I really was, would now be concentrated on the limited patch of country between Beaminster and Lyme Regis.

That part of me which was unconsciously looking after my safety kept count of the minutes (for I dared not stay where I was more than very few) while my conscious mind lived through hours of muddled and panicky thinking. I quite seriously considered taking Saul's advice and telling the police my real name and enough of my trip abroad to account for my disappearance and for the attack upon me in the Aldwych. I forgot that I had worse enemies than the police.

This longing to surrender was very insistent at the time, yet never really came out of the world of dreams. The knowledge that one pack was on my tail had only temporarily excluded fear of the other. There is no animal but man which can be hunted simultaneously by two different packs without the two becoming one; so it is not surprising that all one's sagacity should be at fault.

Reason took over. If I resumed my identity, death or

disgrace was certain. And if some unbalanced idiots chose to regard me as a martyr, I had the makings of a first-class international incident. It was my duty to kill myself – or, easier, arrange for myself to be killed incognito – rather than seek protection.

The police were at the cross-roads ten minutes after I got off the bus. Neither they nor the postmistress's daughter had wasted any time. They switched the headlights of two cars into the spinney where I was, and crashed into the under-growth.

The immediate future didn't worry me at all. It was already dusk, and I knew that in the dark I could pass through a multitude of policemen and possibly take their boots off as well. I moved quietly away in front of them until I had to break cover, either by crossing the road or taking the downs on the west. I didn't want to cross the road – it meant that I should lead the chase into my own country – nor was there any point in stealing away into unknown difficulties. I decided to stay in contact with this lot of police – about five couple of them there were – so I jumped on to the stone wall that bounded the spinney and pretended to remain there indecisively. At last one of them saw me and gave a holloa. I broke away into Devonshire down a long, barren slope.

I was magnificently fit as a result of my life in the open and the brisk autumn air. I remember how easily my muscles answered the call I made on them. By God, in all this immobility and carrion thought it does me good to think of the man I was!

I intended to lie still wherever there was a scrap of not too obvious cover and to let the hunt pass me; but I didn't reckon on a young and active inspector who shed his overcoat and seemed able to do the quarter-mile in well under sixty seconds. As we neared the bottom of the slope, I had no chance of playing hide-and-seek in the gorse or vanishing into a hedge. The lead of a hundred and fifty yards which, in the gathering dusk, I had considered ample for my purpose had been reduced to fifty.

I had to keep running – either for a gate that led into another open field, or a gate beyond which I saw a muddy farm-track with water faintly gleaming in the deep hoof-marks. I chose the mud, and vaulted the gate into eighteen inches of it. I was bogged, but so would he be, and then endurance could count; he wouldn't be able to give me any more of his cinder-track stuff. I pounded along the track, spattering as much mud as a horse over myself and the hedges. He was now twenty yards behind, and wasting his breath by yelling at me to stop and come quietly.

While he was still in the wet clay, and the rest of the police had just entered it, I pulled out on to hard surface. The wall of a farmhouse loomed up ahead; it was built in the usual shape of an E without the centre bar, the house at the back, the barns forming the two wings. It seemed an excellent place for the police to surround and search; they would be kept busy for the next few hours, and the cordon between Lyme Regis and Beaminster, through which I had to pass, would be relaxed.

I looked back. The inspector had dropped back a little; the rest of the hunt I could hear plunging and cursing in the mud. I put on a spurt and dashed round the lower bar of the E. Knowing the general layout of English farms, I was sure that my wanted patch of not too obvious cover would be right at the corner, and it was. I dropped flat on my face in a pattern of mounds and shadows. I couldn't see myself of what they consisted. My head landed in a manure heap with a smell of disinfectant – they had probably been dosing the sheep for worms – and my elbow on an old millstone; there were hurdles and firewood; the dominating shadow was that of an old mounting-block.

The inspector raced round the corner after me and into the open barns, flashing his light on the carts, the piles of fodder and the cider barrels. As soon as he passed me, I shot out of the yard, crouching and silent, and dropped against the outer wall. I hadn't any luck in minor matters. This time I put my face in a patch of nettles.

The police, a full half-minute behind us, dashed into the yard, rallying to their inspector. He was shouting to them to come on boys, that he had the beggar cornered. The farm and its dogs woke up to the fact that there was a criminal in their midst, and I left the police to their search; it was probably long and exhausting, for there was not, from their point of view, the remotest possibility of my escaping from the three-sided trap into which I had run.

I had no intention of going home. There could be no peace for me in the lane until I had laid a false scent and knew that the police were following it to the exclusion of all others.

First: I had to make a false hiding-place and satisfy the police that there I had lived, so that they wouldn't do too thorough a search between Beaminster and Lyme Regis.

Second: I must persuade the police that I had left the district for good.

I followed the main road, along which I had come in the bus, back towards Lyme Regis. I say, I followed it – I had to, since I wasn't sure of my direction in the dark – but I didn't walk on it. I moved parallel, climbing a fence or forcing a hedge about every two hundred yards for three solid miles. It's a major feat of acrobatics to follow a main road without ever setting foot on it, and I began to feel infernally tired.

The high ground to the east of Beaminster, where a new den had to be faked, was twenty miles away. I decided to jump a lorry on the steep hill between Lyme Regis and Charmouth, where I could be pretty sure of getting a lift unknown to the driver.

A mile or so outside the town, I cut down into a valley and up the other side towards the steep hairpin bend where heavy traffic had to slow to walking-pace. I thought this an ingenious and original scheme, but the police, more me-chanically-minded than myself, had thought of it already. At the steepest part of the road was a sergeant with a bicycle, keeping careful watch.

I cursed him heartily and silently, for now I had to go down again to the bottom of the valley, draw him off, and return to the road. My knees were very heavy, but there was nothing else for it. I stood in a little copse at the bottom and started yelling bloody murder in a terrified soprano – 'Help!' and 'Let me go!' and 'God, won't anybody come!' and then a succession of hysterical screams that were horrible to hear and quite false. The screams of a terrified woman are rhythmical and wholly unnatural, and had I imitated them correctly the sergeant would have thought me a ghost or some fool yodelling.

I heard the whine of brakes hastily applied, and several dim figures ran down into the valley as I ran up. I peered over the hedge. The sergeant had gone. A grocer's van and a sports car stood empty by the side of the road. I gave up my original idea of boarding a lorry and took the sports car. I reckoned that I should have the safe use of it for at least twenty-five minutes – ten minutes before the party gave up their search of the wooded bottom, five minutes before they could reach a telephone, and ten more minutes before patrols and police cars could be warned.

Over my head and round my beard I wrapped my muffler. Then I pulled out in front of a noisy milk truck that was banging up the hill, in case the owner should recognize the engine of his own car. It was a fine car. I did the nine twisting miles to Bridport in eleven minutes and ten miles along the Dorchester road in ten minutes. I hated that speed at the time, and I'm ashamed of it. No driver has a right to average more than forty; if he wants to terrify his fellows there are always a few wars going on, and either side will be glad to let him indulge his pleasure and get some healthy exercise at the same time.

Three miles from Dorchester I turned to the left and abandoned the car in a neglected footpath, no wider than itself, between high hedges. I stuck ten pounds in the owner's licence with pencilled apologies (written in block capitals with my left hand) and my sincere hope that the notes would cover his night's lodgings and any incidental loss.

It was now midnight. I crossed the down, slunk unseen round a village and entered the Sydling Valley, which, by the map, appeared to be as remote a dead-end as any in Dorset. I spent the rest of the night in a covered stack, sleeping warmly and soundly between the hay and the corrugated iron. The chances of the police finding the car till daylight were negligible.

After breakfast of blackberries, I struck north along the watershed. There was a main road a quarter of a mile to the west. I watched the posting of constables at two crossings. Down in the valley a police car was racing towards Sydling. They made no attempt to watch the grass tracks, being convinced, I think, that criminals from London never go far from roads. No doubt Scotland Yard had exact statistics showing what my next move would be. My theft of a car had put me into the proper gangster pigeon-hole – from their point of view, a blatant, self-advertising gangster.

The downs on both sides of the Sydling Valley were country after my own heart: patches of gorse and patches of woodland, connected by straggling hedges which gave me cover from the occasional shepherd or farmer but were not thick enough to compel me to climb them. I assumed that all high ground had been picqueted and reckoned – unnecessarily, I expect – on field-glasses as well as eyes.

The valley ended in a great bowl of turf and woodland, crossed by no road, and two miles from the village. Dry bottoms ran up from the head of the valley like the sticks of a fan. In any one of them I might very reasonably have been camping since September.

That which I chose had a wood of hazel on one side and of oak on the other. Between them the brown bracken grew waist high, and through the bracken ran a ride of turf upon which the rabbits were feeding and playing. The glade smelt of fox, turf, and rabbit, the sweet musk that lingers in dry valleys where the dew is heavy and the water flows a few feet underground. The only signs of humanity were two ruined cottages, some bundles of cut hazel rods, and a few cartridge cases scattered about the turf.

On the green track that led to the cottages tall thistles grew unbroken, showing that few ever passed that way. The gardens had been swamped by wild vegetation, but an apple-tree was bearing fruit in spite of the bramble and ivy which grabbed at the low, heavily-laden branches. That invaded tree and garden reminded me of the tropics.

The cottages were roofless, but in one was a hearth that ran two feet back into the thick masonry. I built a rough wall of fallen stone around it, and succeeded in making a fairly convincing nest for a fugitive, drier and more airy than my own but not so safe. While I was working I saw no one but a farmer riding through the bracken on the opposite ridge. I knew what he was looking for – a cow that had just calved. I had run across her earlier in the day, and had been encouraged by this sure sign that the farm was large and full of cover.

When night fell I lit a fire, piling it fiercely up the chimney so that the ash and soot would appear the result of many fires. While it burned I lay in the hazel wood, in case anyone should be attracted by the light and smoke. Then I sat over the ashes dozing and shivering till dawn. I was still wearing my town suit, inadequate for the cold and mist of an October night.

It was hard to make the place look as if I had lived there for weeks. I distributed widely and messily the corpse of a rabbit that was polluting the atmosphere a little way up the valley. I fouled and trampled the interior of the cottage, stripped the apple-tree, and strewed apple-cores and nut-shells over the ground. A pile of feathers from a wood-pigeon and a rook provided further evidence of my diet. Plucking the ancient remains of a hawk's dinner was the nastiest job of all.

I spent the day sitting in the bracken and waiting for the police, but they refused to find me. Possibly they thought that I had made for the coast. There was, after all, no earthly reason why I should be in the Sydling Valley more than anywhere else. I put the night to good use. First I collected a dozen empty tins from a rubbish heap and piled them in a corner of the cottage; then I went down to sleeping Sydling and did a smash-and-grab raid on the village shop. My objects were to draw the attention of those obstinate police, and to get hold of some dried fish. In this sporting country some damned fool was sure to try bloodhounds on my scent.

In the few seconds at my disposal I couldn't find any kippers or bloaters, but I did get four tins of sardines and a small bag of fertilizer. I raced for the downs while the whole village squawked and muttered and slammed its doors. It was probably the first time in all the history of Sydling that a sudden noise had been heard at night.

As soon as I was back in my cottage I pounded the sardines and fertilizer together, tied up the mixture in the bag, and rubbed the corner of the hearth where I had sat and the wall I had built. Trailing the bag on the end of a string, I laid a drag through the hazels, over the heather on the hilltop, round the oak wood, and into the bracken overlooking the cottage. There I remained and got some sleep.

In spite of all the assistance I had given them it was nearly midday before the police discovered the cottages. They moved around in them as respectfully as in church, dusting all likely surfaces for finger-prints. There weren't any. I had never taken off my gloves. They must have thought they were dealing with an experienced criminal.

Half an hour later a police car came bumping over the turf and decanted an old friend of mine into the cottages. I had quite forgotten that he was now Chief Constable of Dorset. If he had looked closely at those feathers he would have seen at once that a hawk, not a man, had done the killing; but naturally he was leaving the criminology to Scotland Yard, and they weren't likely to go into the fine point of whether the birds had met their death through the plumage of back or breast.

The dry bottom began to look like a meet of the Cattistock. The couple of bloodhounds that I had expected turned up, towing a bloodthirsty maiden lady in their wake. She was encouraging them with yawps and had feet so massive that I could see them clearly at two hundred yards

– great brogued boats navigating a green sea. She was followed by half the village of Sydling and a sprinkling of local gentry. Two fellows had turned out on horseback. I felt they should have paid me the compliment of pink coats.

Away went the bloodhounds on the trail of the fertilized sardines, and away I went too; I had a good half hour's law while they followed my bag through the hazels and heather. I crossed the main road – a hasty dash from ditch to ditch while the constable on watch was occupied with the distant beauty of the sea – and slid along the hedges into a great headland of gorse above Cattistock. There I wove so complicated a pattern that boat-footed Artemis must have thought her long-eared darlings were on the line of a hare. I skirted Cattistock and heard their lovely carillon most appropriately chime 'D'ye ken John Peel' at my passage, followed by 'Lead, Kindly Light'. It was half-past five and dusk was falling. I waded into the Frome, passed under the Great Western Railway, and paddled upstream for a mile or so, taking cover in the rushes whenever there was anyone to see me. Then I buried the sardines in the gravel at the bottom of the river, and proceeded under my own scent.

I have not the faintest idea what hounds can or cannot do on the trail of a man. I doubt if they could have run on my true scent from the cottages to my lane, but I had to guard against the possibility. Looking back on those two days, it cheers me to see the healthy insolence in all I did.

I moved slowly westwards, following the lanes but taking no risks – slowly, deliberately slowly, in the technique that I have developed since I became an outlaw. It was nearly four in the morning when I swung myself on to the elm branch that did duty as my front door, and climbed down into the lane. I felt Asmodeus brush against my legs but I could not see him in that safe pit of blackness. That I consider darkness safety sets me, in itself alone, apart from my fellows. Darkness is safety only on condition that all one's enemies are human.

I ate a tremendous breakfast of beef and oatmeal, and set aside my town suit to be made into bags and lashings – all it was now good for. I was relieved to be done with it; it reminded me too forcibly of the newspapers' well-dressed man. Then I slipped into my bag, unwearing, damp-proof citadel of luxury, and slept till nightfall.

When I awoke I felt sufficiently strong and rested to attempt the second feint: to convince the police that I had left the country for good. This was rash, but necessary. I still think it was necessary. If I hadn't gone the bicycle would be in the lane, and the evidence of my presence here a deal stronger than it is.

By the light of two candles – for the battery of the headlamp had run down – I turned to the unholy job of reassembling the tandem. It was after midnight before I had the machine, entire and unpunctured, clear of the lane, and the thorns replaced in a sufficiently forbidding pattern.

I dressed myself in the warmest of my working clothes, tearing off all distinguishing marks and the maker's name. I put a flask of whisky in my inside-breast-pocket, and took plenty of food. I could be away for days without worrying. Even the ventilation hole was no longer suspicious, for Asmodeus used it when the door was jammed home and had given the entrance the proper sandy, claw-worn look. I think he always treated the den as his headquarters in my absence, but, being a cleanly cat, he never left a sign of his tenancy.

I pedalled cautiously through the lanes of the Marshwood Vale and up into the hills beyond. The by-roads were empty. Before crossing any main road I put the bicycle in the hedge and explored on foot and belly. Once I was nearly caught. I crawled almost into a constable whom I mistook, as he towered above me, for a tree-stump. It was the fault of the massive overcoat. The same error, I believe, is frequently made by dogs.

By dawn I was past Crewkerne and well into Somerset. It was now time to let myself be seen and to put the police on a trail that obviously led north to Bristol or some little port on the Bristol Channel. I shot through two scattered villages, where I gave the early risers a sight to look at and talk about for the rest of the day; then on into the Fosse Way, speeding along the arrow-straight road to Bristol and drawing cheers and laughter from the passing lorry-drivers. I was too incredible a sight to be thought a criminal – muddy, bearded, and riding a tandem, as odd a creature as that amusing tramp who used to do tricks on the Halls with a collapsible bicycle.

After showing myself over a mile of main road I was more than ready to hide the bicycle for good and myself till nightfall, but the country on both sides of the great Roman highway was open and unpleasantly short of cover; indeed much of it was below the level of the road. I pedalled on and on in the hope of reaching a wood or heath or quarry. It was all flat land with well-trimmed hedges and shallow drains.

By the side of the road was an empty field of cabbages – one of those melancholy fields with a cinder track leading into it and a tumbledown hut leaning against a pile of refuse. Close to the hut and at a stone's throw from the road was a derelict car. When the only traffic was a cluster of black dots a mile or two away, I lifted the tandem on to my shoulder, to avoid leaving a track, and staggered into the shelter of the hut. I smashed the two sets of handle-bars so that the bicycle would lie flat on the ground, and shoved it under the car, afterwards restoring the trampled weeds to a fairly upright position. It will not be found until the car moulders away above it, and then it will be indistinguishable from the other rusty debris.

I now had to take cover myself. The hut was too obvious a place. The hedges were inadequate. I dared not risk so much as a quarter-mile walk. There was nothing for it but to lie on the clay among those blasted cabbages. In the middle of the field I was perfectly safe.

It was a disgusting day. The flats of England on a grey morning remind me of the classical hell – a featureless landscape where the peewits twitter and the half-alive remember hills and sunshine. And the asphodel of this Hades is the cabbage. To lie among cabbages in my own country should have been nothing after the pain and exposure I suffered during my escape; but it was summer then and it was autumn now. To lie still on a clay soil in a gentle drizzle was exasperating. But safe! If the owner of that vile field had been planting, he'd have stuck his dibber into me before noticing that I wasn't mud.

I was so bored that I was thankful when in the early afternoon a car stopped at the gate into the field, and a party of three policemen crunched up the cinder path. I had been expecting them for hours; they knew that I had been seen on the Fosse Way in the morning, and since then nowhere, so it was certain they would search every possible hiding-place along the highway and its by-roads. They looked into the hut and into that decaying car. I kept my face well down between my arms, so I don't know whether they even glanced at the cabbage field. Probably not. It was so open and innocent.

I shivered and grumbled for an eternity in that repellant field. I tried to find comfort in infinitesimal changes of position; there was none to be had, but it occupied my mind to change, for example, my head from elbow to forearm or to twist my feet from resting on the ankles to resting on the insteps. I analysed the comparative discomforts of the various movements open to me. I made patterns out of the avenues of cabbages that spread in a quadrant before my eyes. I tortured myself (for even torture may be a diversion) by thinking of the flask of whisky in my inner breast-pocket and refusing to allow myself to touch it. I knew damn well that I dared not touch it; the wriggles necessary to get at it and the flash of the nickel-plate might have given me away. There were plenty of cars and cyclists on the road, and the owner of the field, presumably advised that his hut had received a visit from the police, was leaning against it in the company of two friends and looking over his possessions with ruminative pride. I don't suppose there had been so much excitement in the villages since Monmouth's troops were flying from Sedgemoor, foundering their horses in that awful plough-land, and crawling in the muck like me and the worms.

At last the cabbage-man went home to his soggy tea, and dusk fell and I stood up. I drank a quarter of my flask and struck eastwards away from the road. Cross-country travel in the dark was nearly impossible. I felt my way along drains and hedges, usually circumnavigating three sides of a field before I found the way out of it – and when I did find the way out, it invariably led me into a village or back into the cabbage field.

After an hour or two of this maze, I struck straight across country, climbing or wading whatever obstacles were in my way. This was sheer obstinacy. I was wet to the armpits; I was leaving a track like a hippopotamus; and, since I didn't know where I was heading, it was all objectless. Finally, I took to the lanes – or roads, I should call them, for they were narrow ribbons of tarmac with low hedges. There I spent most of the time pretending to be a manure heap, for the roads were relatively crowded with pedestrians. The average was certainly one person for every two hundred yards. Evening entertainment in that dreary vale consists of pub-crawling to the next village and back again. If you haven't the money for beer, you lie under a mackintosh with a girl. At normal times I have only sympathy for so firm an attachment to the preliminaries of procreation, but the groups by the wayside were not recognizable as human until I had practically stepped on them. My own county is gayer and more pagan. When it rains we do our love-making in the tithe barn or the church porch or under the steps at the back of the Women's Institute, and we don't care who sees us. Trespassers are expected to guffaw and look away.

I should have been forced to spend another day in the cabbage field if I had not stumbled across a railway line which I followed towards Yeovil, stepping quietly from sleeper to sleeper. Two railway employees passed me walking homewards, but their boots on the ballast gave me ample warning of their approach. I avoided them, and the one train, by lying down at the bottom of the embankment.

A denser darkness on the horizon warned me that I was nearing the massed little houses of Yeovil. It was then about two in the morning, and the by-roads were deserted; so I turned south towards the hills. When the slow autumn dawn turned night to mist I could feel the short turf under my feet and see the gleam of chalk and flint wherever man or beast had scraped the escarpment.

I drank at the piped spring which fed a cattle-trough and took refuge in the heart of a wild half-acre of gorse and heather. Here I startled an old dog fox, and startled myself, when I came to consider it, a deal more. I flatter myself I am able to get as near to game as any civilized man and most savages; indeed it has been my favourite pursuit since I was given my first air-rifle at the age of six, and told – an injunction which, with a single exception, I have obeyed – that I must never point a gun at anyone. Yet I should certainly not have backed myself to approach within three yards of a fox, even knowing where he was and deliberately stalking him. Oddly enough, it worried me that I had come to move with such instinctive quietness. I was already on the look-out for all signs of demoralization – morbidly anxious to assure myself that I was losing none of my humanity.

I chose a south bank where short heather was gradually overcoming the turf, laying back springs under its green mattress. The sun promised a mild heat, and I spread out my coat and leather jacket to dry. I dozed sweetly, awakening whenever a bird perched on the gorse or a rabbit scuttered through the runways, but instantly and easily falling asleep again.

A little after midday I woke up for good. There was nothing immediately visible to account for the sudden clarity of my senses, so I peered over the gorse. Up wind were two men strolling along the crest of the hill. One was a sergeant of the Dorset constabulary; the other a small farmer – to judge by the fact that he carried an old-fashioned hammer-gun. They passed me within ten yards, the policeman pressing down with firm feet as if searching for a pavement beneath that silent and resilient turf, the farmer plodding along with the slightly bent knees of a man who seldom walks on the flat.

I decided to follow these two solemn wanderers and hear what they had to say. They were discussing me, since the farmer had remarked, apropos of nothing: ''Tis my belief he was over to Zumerset all the time' – a final and definite pronouncement as of one who should say: I believe he went to South America and died there.

It's curious how much cover there is on the chalk downs. A body of men couldn't move unseen, but a single man can. In the vales of southern England, though they look like woodland from the top of hills, hedges and fences compel the fugitive to go the way of other men, and sooner or later he is forced, as I was, to lie down and pray for the earth to cover him. But on the bare – apparently bare – downs there are prehistoric pits and trenches, tree-grown stumps, gorse and the upper edge of coverts, lonely barns and thickets of thorn. And the hedges, where there are any, are either miniature forests or full of gaps.

It was easy to catch them up. They went at an easy pace, stopping every now and then to exchange a few words. The weighty business of conversation could not be disturbed by movement. At last they settled on a gate and leaned over it, contemplating twenty acres of steely green mangel-wurzels which sloped down to the golden hedges of the vale. I crawled the length of a dry ditch and came within earshot.

The sergeant finished a long mumble with the word 'foreigners', pronounced loudly and aggressively.

"Err, they bastards!' said the farmer.

The sergeant considered this judicially, turning with deliberation towards his companion and me. He was a uniformed servant of the State, and thus, I imagine, predisposed to diplomacy.

'I wouldn't 'ardly go so far as that,' he said. 'Not that I 'old with furr'ners – but I don't know as I'd go so far as that.'

There was a deal more conversation which I couldn't hear, because neither of them was sufficiently excited to raise his voice. The farmer, I think, must have denied that any foreigners ever came to Dorset. The suggestion that they did was almost a criticism on his county.

'I tell 'ee there's been furr'ners askin' for 'm,' said the sergeant. 'And I knows that, because the inspector says to me, 'e says . . .' then his voice trailed away again.

'Mrs Maydoone says 'e were a proper gent,' chuckled the farmer.

The sergeant chuckled in sympathy and then showed offended dignity.

'Told me she couldn't 'ardly call 'im to mind, she did! Don't 'ee come asking questions, she says, as if the Bull were a nasty common public-'ouse, she says.'

There was more laughter, which turned to a full-throated giggle as both remembered the opulent Mrs Maydoone and dug each other in their own less admirably covered ribs. She was a respectably eager widow who owned the inn in Beaminster where I had lunched. The doctors, she told me, had never seen anything like Mr Maydoone's kidneys outside a London hospital.

My two friends marched off across the downs, while I remained in the ditch digesting the scraps of news. I was perturbed, but not surprised. It was natural enough that my enemies should get possession of Scotland Yard's clue to my whereabouts. If dear old Holy George couldn't manage it, then one of their newspaper correspondents in London could. It wasn't confidential information.

I returned to my form in the heart of the gorse. The early afternoon sun had a dying bite of summer in it, and I was glowing with the exertion of my stalk. At dusk I ate the last of my provisions and drank again at the spring. By good fortune I left untouched the half-flask of whisky that remained. I feared its effect – slight, but enough to give me confidence, when my safe return to the lane and my peace of mind throughout the winter depended on moving now with the utmost caution.

I kept to the hill-tops, following the ridgeways southwards till they ended on Eggardon Down. There I was lost. There was not a star showing, and although I knew I was on Eggardon, I could not tell from what point of the compass I had immediately approached it; the tracks, ancient and modern, green and metalled, crossed and switched like the lines in a goods yard. At last I found myself in the outer ditch of the camp and, to make sure of my orientation, walked half-way round the huge circuit of earthworks until I could see far below me the faint lights of a town, which had to be Bridport.

The emptiness was infinity, darkness with distance but no shape. The south-west wind swirled over the turf, and the triple line of turf ramparts hung over me like smooth seas travelling through the night. I might have been upon the eastern slopes of the Andes with an empty continent of forest at my feet. I could have wished it so. There I should have felt alone, secure, an impregnable outpost of humanity.

Eggardon affected me as a city. The camp was haunted. I didn't feel the presence of its builders, those unknown imperialists who set their cantonments on the high chalk, but I was suddenly terrified of the sleeping towns and villages that lay at my feet and clustered, waiting, around empty Eggardon. A grey mare and her foal leaped monstrously out of a ditch and galloped away. A thorn-bush just beyond the easy range of sight hovered between reality and a vision; it was round and black like the mouth of a tunnel. Guilt was on me. I had killed without object, and my fellows were all around me waiting lest I should kill again.

I stumbled down to the valley, compelling myself to move

slowly and to look straight ahead. If there had been any living being upon Eggardon I should have walked into him. I was obsessed by this sense of all southern England crowding in upon the hill.

As I dodged and darted home from lane to lane and farmhouse to farmhouse, I couldn't get the side-car out of my head. I wanted to know if it had been disturbed. Should the police have found it, and taken it from the stream for identification, they might disbelieve the evidence of the cottages – which was good only as long as no one questioned it – and search the country where I really was.

Although it was only a field away from a well-frequented by-road, the side-car was in a safe place: a muddy little stream flowing between deep banks with the hawthorn arching overhead. It would remain unseen, I thought, for years unless some yokel took it into his head to wade up the bed of the stream or a cow rubbed her way through the bushes.

I entered the water at a cattle-wallow, plunging up to my knees in mire, and forced my way under the hawthorn. I couldn't see the side-car. I was sure of the place, but it wasn't there. I didn't allow myself to worry yet, but I felt, as a stab of pain, the cold of the water. I pushed on downstream, hoping that the side-car had been shifted by the force of the current, and knowing very well, as I now remember, that nothing but a winter flood would shift it.

At last I saw it, a faint white bulk in the darkness canted up against a bank of rushes where the stream widened. I was so glad to find it that I didn't hesitate, didn't listen to the intuition that was clamouring to be heard, and being ascribed to nervousness. After Eggardon I was not allowing any imagination any play.

I was leaning over the side-car when a voice quite softly called my name. I straightened up, so astounded and fascinated that for a second I couldn't move. A thin beam of light flashed on my face, and dropped to my heart with a roar and a smashing blow. I was knocked backwards across the baby carriage, pitching with my right side on the mud and my head half under water. I have no memory of falling, only of the light and the simultaneous explosion. I must have been unconscious while I hit the mud, for just so long, I suppose, as my heart took to recover its habit of beating.

I remained collapsed, with eyes staring, trying to pick up the continuity of life. If I had had the energy I should have cackled with crazy laughter; it seemed so very extraordinary to have a beam of light thrust through one's heart and be still alive. I heard my assassin give his ridiculous party war-cry in a low, fervent voice, as if praising God for the slaughter of the infidel. Then a car cruised quietly up the road, and I heard a door slam as someone got out. I lay still, uncertain whether the gunman had gone to meet the newcomer or not; he had, for I heard their voices a moment later as they approached the stream, presumably to collect my body. I crawled off through the grass and rushes on the far bank, and bolted for home. I am not ashamed to remember that I was frightened, shocked, careless. To be shot from ambush is horribly unnerving.

I jumped into my tree and down into the lane, regardless of darting pain whenever I moved my right arm. Then I shut the door of the den behind me and lay down to collect myself. When I had regained a more graceful mastery of my spirit, I lit a candle and explored the damage.

The bullet – from a .45 revolver – had turned on the nickel of the flask in my breast-pocket, ploughed sideways through my leather jacket and come to rest (point foremost, thank God!) in the fleshy part of my right shoulder. It was so near the surface that I squeezed it out with my fingers. The skin was bruised and broken right across my chest, and I felt as if I had been knocked down by a railway engine; but no serious damage had been done.

I understood why the hunter had not even taken the trouble to examine his kill. He had shot along the beam of a flash-lamp, seen the bullet strike and watched the stain of whisky, which couldn't in artificial light be distinguished from blood, leap to the breast of my coat and spread. It wasn't necessary to pay me any further attention for the moment; he had no use for my pelt or liver.

I patched myself up and lit a pipe, thinking of the fellow who had shot me. He had used a revolver because a rifle couldn't be handled in such thick cover and at so close a range, but his technique showed that he had experience of big-game. He had got into my mind. He knew that sooner or later I should have a look at that side-car. And his gentle calling of my name to make me turn my head was perfect.

They had despatched a redoubtable emissary. He knew, as the police did not, who I was and what sort of man I was; thus he had been suspicious of my elaborate false trails. He guessed the plain facts: that I had committed a folly in going to Lyme Regis, and that my jack-in-the-box tricks thereafter were evidence of nothing but my anxiety. Therefore I had some secure hiding-place not far from Lyme Regis and almost certainly on the Beaminster side of it. His private search for the side-car, which he may have been carrying on for weeks, was then concentrated on the right spot. That he found it was due to imagination rather than luck. It had to be near a track or lane; it was probably in wood or water. And I think if I had been he I should have voted for water. There was a pattern in my escape. I had a preference for hiding, travelling, throwing off pursuit by water. Water, as the Spanish would say, was my *querencia*.

Well, he had missed. I think I wrote in some other context which I have forgotten that the Almighty looks after the rogue male. Nevertheless this sportsman (I allow him the title, for he must have waited up two or three nights over his bait, and been prepared to wait for many more) would be content. He had discovered the bit of country where I had been hiding, and he could even be pretty sure whereabouts my lair was. My panic-stricken dash through the water-meadow showed that I was bolting south. I wouldn't be camping in the marshland; therefore the only place for me was on or just over the semicircle of low hills beyond. All that he had to do was to go into the long grass, as it were, after his wounded beast. The hunt had narrowed from all England to Dorset, from Dorset to the western corner of the county, and from that to four square miles.

I had known that this fate, whether delayed for months or years, was on the way to me; but the tranquillity of my life in the lane had taken the edge off my fear. I had been inclined to brood over my motives and congratulate myself on my superior cleverness, to look back rather than forward. There is, indeed, nothing to look forward to, no activities, no object; so I clung, and clung to what I have – this lane. I might have escaped and lived on the country, but sooner or later one pack or the other would run me to earth, and no earth could be so deep and well-disguised as this.

It was obvious that, if I stayed where I was, I must completely reverse my policy of keeping the lane closed. The thorns must go, and the place be wide open to inspection while I myself lived underground.

I started on the work immediately. A south-west gale was sweeping down the hillside carrying along with it a solid ceiling of cloud high enough for the rain to drive and sting, so low that the whole sky seemed in movement. I welcomed the rain, for it helped me to obliterate all trace of myself and it would discourage the two men in the car from attempting to follow me up until visibility was better.

The eastern hedge, beneath which my burrow ran, was as wide as a cottage and promised to be as impenetrable in winter as in summer. The western hedge, however, which bounded the ploughed field, had not been allowed to eat up so much land and formed a thinner screen. I built up the weak stretches, thus getting rid of the poles from my platform and a lot of loose brushwood. The holly bush and the larger branches of thorn I shoved into the eastern hedge, hiding the cut ends. I stamped the earth hard down over my rubbish pit, and the water that was now rushing along the bottom of the lane covered pit and floor with a smooth expanse of dead bracken and red sand. I then retired indoors, leaving it to the rain to wash out my foot prints. I have never had a chance to dry the clothes in which I was working.

The obliteration was not perfect. Bracken and nettles were crushed, but, since the whole lane was filled with the dying debris of autumn, the traces of my tramplings and removals were not very plain. There was a faint but definite smell. Worst of all, there were the steps cut up the inside of the elm which could not be disguised. If the fellow who was about to go into the covert after me had an observant eye – and I knew he had – he was bound to consider the lane suspicious; but I hoped he would judge his suspicions wrong and conclude that, whether or not I had once lived between the hedges, I had taken to the open and died of my wound.

The door was a faultless piece of camouflage; I had planted around it the same weeds as were over it, and no one could tell which had died with their roots in earth and which with their roots in glue. A few trails of living ivy hung over the door from the hedge.

Thenceforth my way out of the burrow was the chimney. The diameter of its course through the solid sandstone was already sufficient to receive my body; only the last ten feet of broken stone and earth had to be widened. I completed the job that afternoon – a nightmarish job, for my shoulder was painful and I was continually knocking off to rest. Then I would begin to dream of the root or the stone or the water that was beating me, and I would get up again and go to work, half naked and foul with the red earth, a creature inhuman in mind and body. I think that sometimes I must have worked while asleep. It was the first time that I experienced this dazed and earthly dreaming; it has since become very common.

A queer tunnel it seemed to me when I examined it after a night's sleep. I hadn't attempted to cut through any roots that were thicker than a thumb; I had gone round them. At one point I had tunnelled right away from the chimney, and come back to it. This was all to the good. Though the curve demanded odd contortions to get in and out, the roots acted as the rungs of a ladder, and the slope as a sump for water. The mouth was still well hidden under the blackberry bush. The only disaster was that my inner chamber was now full of wet earth, and I have no means of dumping it elsewhere.

God! When I look back upon them those blind hours of work seem to have been happy in spite of all their muddy and evasive horror. I had something to do. Something to do. There is no fearing dreams when they produce work. It is when they feed upon themselves that one becomes uncertain of reality, unable to distinguish between the present in one's mind and the present as it appears to the outer world.

I stared at my face today, hoping to see those spiritual attributes which surprised me when I first looked in the fisherman's mirror. I wanted comfort from my face, wanted to know that this torture, like the last, had refined it. I saw my eyes fouled with earth, my hair and beard dripping with blood-red earth, my skin grey and puffed as that of a crushed earthworm. It was the mask of a beast in its den, terrified, waiting.

But I must not anticipate. To preserve my sanity it is necessary that I take things in their order. That is the object of this confession: to tell things in their order, reasonably, precisely: to recover that man with his insolence, his irony, his ingenuity. By writing of him I become him for the time.

It was Major Quive-Smith who had shot me by the stream. I am sure of it because his subsequent behaviour and his character (which by now I know as an old fox, outliving his contemporaries, knows the idiosyncrasies of the huntsman) correspond to those of the man who waited patiently over the side-car, who called my name to make me turn my head.

Two days I spent recovering from the wound, light in itself but aggravated by all that sudden toil. On the third I emerged from my chimney and crawled from bush to bush along the edge of the eastern pasture until I reached an ivy-covered oak at the bottom of the lane. It was nearly dead, and a paradise of wood-pigeons. From the top I could see the Marshwood Vale spread out as on a map, and I overlooked the courtyard of Patachon's farm.

Pat and Patachon are the names I have given to my two neighbours. I live unsuspected between them like an evil spirit, knowing their ways and their characters but not permitted to discover their true names. Pat, the farmer to whom the cows and the eastern hedge belong, is a tall, thin youth with a lined, brown face, a habit of muttering to himself, and a soul embittered by bad home-made cider. His little dairy farm can barely pay its way; but he has an active wife with a lot of healthy poultry, which probably produce all the ready cash. On the other hand she is prolific as her hens. They have six children with expensive tastes. I judge the kids by the fact that they suck sweets at the same time as eating blackberries.

Patachon, who owns the western hedge and the great grey farm, is a chunky, red-faced old rascal, always with a tall ash-plant in his hand when he hasn't a gun. His terse Dorset speech delights his labourers, and is heard, I should guess, on a number of local boards. His land runs past the lower end of the lane, and round over the top of the hill, so that Pat's pasture is an enclave in the middle of it. On warm evenings he walks his side of the hedge in the hope of picking up rabbit or wood-pigeon, but the only shots he has ever fired were at Asmodeus. The old poacher was too quick for him; all you can do to Asmodeus is to shoot where he ought to be but never is.

All morning I saw nothing of interest from the tree, but in the afternoon two men in a car drove into the yard of Patachon's farm and dropped a bag and a gun-case. Then they bumped along the lower edge of the stubble, following the farm track which joined the serviceable portion of my lane. I guessed that they must be bound for Pat's farm; if they had been going beyond it, they would have taken a better road. I couldn't keep them under observation, for the southern slopes were much too dangerous in daylight. There were deep lanes which had to be crossed or entered, with no possibility of avoiding other pedestrians.

In half an hour they were back at Patachon's. One of the men got out and went indoors. The other drove the car away. Someone, then, had come to stay at the farm. I remained on watch in the tree, for I didn't like the look of things.

In the evening Patachon and his visitor emerged from the farmhouse with their guns under their arms, prepared for a stroll round the estate. They started towards the low-lying thickets at the western end of the farm, and I didn't see them again for an hour. Patachon owned a lot of rough land in that direction which I had never bothered to explore. I heard a few shots. A flight of three duck shot northwards and vanished in the dusk. A wood-pigeon came homing to my tree, saw me, banked against the wind and dived side-ways with brilliant virtuosity. When I caught sight of the two guns again, they were stealing along the edge of the lane, separated from me only by the width of the two hedges. Patachon's visitor was Major Quive-Smith.

The farmer picked up a stone and flung it smack into the tree, just missing my feet. No pigeon flew out of the ivy, needless to say.

'And if 'e'd a bin there,' said Patachon bitterly, ' 'e'd a flewed t'other way.'

'He would,' agreed Major Quive-Smith. 'By Jove! I can't think why that fellow wouldn't let his little bit of shooting!'

That explained why he had gone to see Pat. And Pat, I am sure, refused his request rudely and finally.

'Sour man, 'e is!' said the farmer. 'Sour!'

'Does he shoot at all himself?'

'No. 'E baint a man for fun. But don't 'ee go botherin' 'im, Major, for there's nobbut in the 'edge this year.'

'How's that?' asked Quive-Smith.

I could see the swift, suspicious turn of his head, and hear the bark in the question.

'A perishin' cat! Can't trap 'un. Can't shoot 'un.'

'Very shy of man, I suppose?'

'Knows as well as we what us would do to 'un if us could catch 'un,' Patachon agreed.

They strolled down to the farm for supper. I observed that the major carried one of those awkward German weapons with a rifled barrel below the two gun barrels. As a rifle, it is inaccurate at 200 yards; as a gun, unnecessarily heavy. But the three barrels were admirably adapted to his purpose of ostensibly shooting rabbits while actually expecting bigger game.

I don't yet know Quive-Smith's true nationality or name. As a retired military man he had nearly, but not quite, convinced Saul. In his present part, a nondescript gentleman amusing himself with a farm holiday and some cheap and worthless shooting, there was no fault to be found. Tall, fair, slim, and a clever actor, he could pass as a member of half a dozen different nations according to the way he cut his hair and moustache. His cheekbones are too high to be typically English, but so are my own. His nose is that unmistakable Anglo-Roman which with few exceptions – again I am one of them – seems to lead its possessor to Sandhurst. He might have been a Hungarian or Swede, and I have seen faces and figures like his among fair-haired Arabs. I think he is not of pure European origin; his hands, feet, and bone structure are too delicate.

To rent the shooting over three-quarters of the country where I was likely to be was a superb conception. He had every right to walk about with a gun and to fire it. If he bagged me, the chances were a thousand to one against the murder ever being discovered. In a year or two Saul would have to assume that I was dead. But where had I died? Anywhere between Poland and Lyme Regis. And where was my body? At the bottom of the sea or in a pit of quick-lime if Quive-Smith and his unknown friend with the car knew their business.

I was glad of my two unconscious protectors: Asmodeus, whose presence in the lane made my own rather improbable, and Pat who wouldn't have trespassers on his land and wouldn't let his little bit of shooting. I know that type of dyspeptic John Bull. When he has forbidden a person to enter his ground, he is ready to desert the most urgent jobs merely to watch his boundary fence. Quive-Smith couldn't be prevented from exploring Pat's side of the hedge, but he would have to do it with discretion and preferably at night.

I returned to my burrow, now no larger than it had been in the first few weeks, and much damper. I cursed myself for not having widened the chimney before I cleaned up the lane; I could then have thrown out the earth and allowed the rain to distribute it. The inner chamber was uninhabitable and so remains.

I stayed in my sleep-bag for two wretched days. I envied Quive-Smith. He was showing great courage in hunting single-handed a fugitive whom he believed to be desperate. Twice Asmodeus came home with a rush through the ventilation hole and crouched at the back of the den, untouchable and malignant – a sure sign that somebody was in the lane. I lay still underground. Desperate I was, and am, but I want no violence.

On the third afternoon I found the immobility and dirt no longer endurable, and decided to reconnoitre. Asmodeus was out, so I knew that there was no human being in the immediate vicinity. I hoped that Quive-Smith was already paying attention to some other part of the county, or at least to some other farm, but I warned myself not to under-estimate his patience. I poked my filthy head and shoulders out into the heart of the blackberry bush and remained there, listening. It was a long and intricate process to leave the bush; I had to lie flat on the ground, separating the trailing stems with gloved hands and pushing myself forwards with my toes.

I sat among my green fortifications, enjoying the open air and watching Pat's field and the sheep down beyond. It wasn't much to have under observation. Behind me was my own lane, and fifty yards to my left the cross hedge in which was another lane running up to the down; there might have been a platoon of infantry in both, for all that I could have seen of them or they of me. Opposite me was another hedge that separated Pat's pasture from Patachon's sheep; to my right, the skyline of the pasture.

About five o'clock Pat came into the field to drive the cows home himself – a task that hitherto he had always left to a boy – and remained for some time staring about him truculently and swinging a stick. At sunset Major Quive-Smith detached himself from a brown-scarred rabbit warren on the hillside, and put his field-glasses back in their case. I had not the remotest notion that he was there, but, since I had been assuming he was everywhere, I knew he had not seen me. To let me see him I thought obliging.

He struck down the hillside into the lane leading to Patachon's farm. As soon as he was in dead ground I crawled to the corner to have a look at him while he passed beneath me. A clump of gorse covered me from observation from the pasture as I crouched in the angle of the hedges.

I waited but he didn't come. Then it occurred to me that he must hate those deep tracks almost as much as I did; a man walking along them was completely at the mercy of anyone above him. So he was possibly behind the opposite hedge, working his way back to the farm across the fields. It seemed odd that he should take all that trouble when he could have gone home by the vale and run no risks whatever; it seemed so odd that I suddenly realized I had been out-manoeuvred. He had shown himself deliberately.

If I were haunting the lane, which he suspected, and out for revenge, of which he must have been sure, then I should have waited for him just in that corner where I was.

I turned round and peered through the gorse. He was racing silently down the slope towards me. He had decoyed me into the corner of two hedges, from which there was no escape.

He hadn't seen me. He didn't know I was there; he could only hope I was there. I tried a desperate bluff.

'Git off my land!' I yelled. 'Git off ut, I tell 'ee, or I'll 'ave the law on 'ee!'

It was a good enough imitation of Pat's high-pitched voice, but it wasn't very good Dorset. However, I speak my county dialect as richly as my old nurse, and we're near enough to the Bristol Channel to have the west-country burr. I hoped Quive-Smith had not learned to distinguish between one dialect and another.

The major stopped in his stride. It was quite possible that Pat was standing in the lane and looking at him through the hedge, and he didn't want to quarrel more than could be helped.

'Go round by t' ga-ate, and git off my land!' I shouted.

'I say, I'm very sorry!' said Quive-Smith in a loud and embarrassed military voice – he was acting his part.

He turned, and strolled back up the field with offended dignity. I did not even wait for him to reach the skyline, for he might have lain down and continued observation. I sprinted along the twenty yards of straight hedge between the gorse and my own bramble patch, wriggled under the blackberry bush and popped into my burrow. I remained till nightfall with my head and shoulders above ground, but heard no more of him.

I have a reasonable certainty that Quive-Smith will never discover the deception. Pat is sure to be rude and taciturn in any conversation. If the major apologizes when they next meet, Pat will accept the apologies with a grunt, and, if asked straight out whether or not he ordered the major off his land on such a day at such an hour, will allow it to be thought he did. My presence in the lane is still not proven. Suspected, yes. Before Quive-Smith got home to supper, he had no doubt kicked himself for not walking right up to the angle of the hedges.

How much did he know? He had decided, obviously, that I had not been badly wounded; I had, after all, left the stream at a pace that defied pursuit, and there had not been a spot of blood. Then where was I? He had, I presumed, explored all the cover on Patachon's farm and on the two or three others over which he was shooting. He had found no trace of me except in the lane, and he knew that at some time it had been my headquarters. Was I still there? No, but I might return; the lane was well worth watching until the police or the public reported me elsewhere.

His general routine was more or less predictable. If he made a habit of scouting around Pat's pasture in daylight, he ran a real risk of being assaulted or sued for trespass, and he had at all costs to avoid drawing attention to himself by a large local row. By day, then, he might be on the high ground or in the lane itself or on Patachon's side of it. After dusk he would explore or lie up in the pasture.

I was confident that, under these circumstances, he would not find the mouth of my earth, but on one condition – that I cleaned it up and never used it again. There must not be a stem of the bush out of place, nor a blade of grass bent nor any loose earth scraped from my clothes.

I resigned myself to remaining in the burrow, however

unendurable. I have determined not to give way to impatience. I have been underground for nine days.

I dare not smoke or cook, but I have plenty of food: a large store of nuts and most of the tinned meat and groceries that I brought back from my last trips to Beaminster. Of water I have far more than I need. It collects in the sandstone channels that run like wainscoting along the sides of the den and slops over on to the floor. Lest it should undermine the door I have driven two holes, half an inch in diameter, through to the lane, drilling with a tin-opener attached to the end of a stick. I keep them plugged during the day for fear that Quive-Smith might notice such unnatural springs.

Space I have none. The inner chamber is a tumbled morass of wet earth which I am compelled to use as a latrine. I am confined to my original excavation, the size of three large dog-kennels, where I lie on or inside my sleeping-bag. I cannot extend it. The noise of working would be audible in the lane.

I spend a part of each day wedged in the enlarged chimney, with my head out of the top; but that is more for change of position than for fresh air. The domed, prolific bush is so thick and so shadowed by its companions and by the hedge that I can be sure it is day only when the sun is in the east. The lifeless centre seems full of gases, unsatisfying in themselves and carrying in suspension the brown dust and debris that fall from above and the soot from my fires that has accumulated on the under side of the leaves.

Asmodeus, as always, is my comfort. It is seldom that one can give to and receive from an animal close, silent, and continuous attention. We live in the same space, in the same way, and on the same food, except that Asmodeus has no use for oatmeal, nor I for field-mice. During the hours while he sits cleaning himself, and I motionless in my dirt, there is, I believe, some slight thought transference between us. I cannot 'order' or even 'hope' that he should perform a given act, but back and forth between us go thoughts of fear and disconnected dreams of action. I should call these dreams madness, did I not know they came from him and that his mind is, by our human standards, mad.

All initiative is at an end. All luck is at an end. We are so dependent on luck, good and bad. I think of those men and women – cases faintly parallel to mine – who live in one room and eat poorly and lie in bed, since their incomes are too small for any marked activity. Their lives would be unbearable were it not for their hopes of good luck and fears of bad. They have, in fact, little of either; but illusion magnifies what there is.

I have no chance even of illusion. Luck has reached a state of equilibrium and stopped. I had one stroke of evil when that trailer innocently attracted the notice of the police, one stroke of magnificent luck when Quive-Smith's bullet hit the flask. In most other cases I have been able to account for the march of events by conscious planning or by my own instinctive and animal reactions under stress.

Now luck, movement, wisdom, and folly have all stopped. Even time has stopped, for I have no space. That, I think, is the reason why I have again taken refuge in this confession. I retain a sense of time, of the continuity of a stream of facts. I remind myself that I have extended and presumably will extend again in the time of the outer world. At present I exist only in my own time, as one does in a nightmare, forcing myself to a fanaticism of endurance. Without a God, without a love, without a hate – yet a fanatic! An embodiment of that myth of foreigners, the English gentleman, the gentle Englishman, I will not kill; to hide I am ashamed. So I endure without object.

have a use for this record, so I finish it. By God, it is good to write with a purpose, good to grudge the time I must spend on it, instead of whining, as it were, up my own sleeve! This will not, I think, be a pleasant task, nor dispassionate. But I can and must be frank.

I remained in my burrow for eleven days – for a week because it was a week, for two more days to prove to myself that I was not being unduly impatient, and still two more for good measure. Eleven days seemed ample to persuade Quive-Smith that I had either died in cover or left the district; I was entitled to find out whether he had gone. Asmodeus' behaviour suggested that he had. For the middle days the cat had been coming and going in dignified leisure, his ears upright and the hair along his back unruffled. For the last three I had not seen him at all. His delicate movements made the reason perfectly clear; he could not endure the dirt any longer.

Without climbing a tree or exposing myself on open ground – both too dangerous – it was impossible to spy on Quive-Smith during the day; so I decided to look for him after nightfall in the farm itself. Inch by inch I emerged from the blackberry bush and crawled on my stomach to the hedge at the top of Pat's pasture, then through it and over the close turf of the down to much the same point that the major himself had occupied. It was cold and very dark, with a slight ground mist; I was quite safe so long as I moved slowly and avoided the lanes. It was very heaven to be out on the grass and breathing. A blazing summer noon couldn't have given me more pleasure than that foul November night.

There was little wind. The countryside was utterly silent except for the drop of the trees. I could see the lights in Patachon's farm and smell the sweet wood smoke from his chimneys. I dropped down into the vale and made my way to the farm along the edge of the open road, coming to the back of the north wing across an orchard. Here there was a high wall with the sloping roof of a farm building above it. From the top of the gable I should have the yard and the whole front of the house under observation. I didn't care to enter the yard itself. Even if the dogs neither heard nor saw me, the south-west wind, such as it was, would have carried my scent to them.

The wall was built of flints and easily climbed, but there was a gap of two feet between the top of the wall and the lower edge of the slates which gave me trouble. A rotten iron gutter ran below the slates, and it was difficult to reach the roof without momentarily putting some weight on this gutter. Eventually I got up by way of a stout iron bracket and the gable end.

I lay on the slates with my head over the coping. I could see right into the living-room of the farm – a peaceful and depressing sight. Quive-Smith was playing chess with Patachon's small daughter. I was surprised to see him sitting so carelessly before a lighted window with the blind up, and all black Dorset outside; but then I understood that, as always, I had underrated him. The clever devil knew that he was safe with his head nearly touching that of the child across the board. He was teaching her the game. I saw him laugh and shake his head and show her some move she should have made.

It was a bitter shock to find him still there. The eleven days had seemed an eternity to me. To him they were just eleven days; it was even possible, I thought, that he had been enjoying himself. My disappointment turned to fury. It was the first time in the whole of this business that I lost my temper. I lay on the roof picking at the moss on the stone coping, and cursing Quive-Smith, his country, his party, and his boss in a white-hot silence. I blasted him to hell, him and his friends and Patachon and their manservants and maid-servants. If my thoughts had hit those walls, I should have created a massacre that would have done credit to a plunging Jehovah called from eternity by the anathemas of a thousand infuriated priests.

It shook me out of my melancholy, that blazing, silent orgasm of rage. I didn't stop to think that I had brought all this on myself, nor to consider that if I had actually been transported to that living-room I should have shown a damned silly punctilious courtesy to the lot of them. I let myself go. I don't remember anything like it since I enjoyed – certainly, enjoyed – speechless temper at the age of seven.

I was brought back to reality by a fit of shivering. I had sweated with wrath and the perspiration was cooling in the night air. It's strange that I noticed it, for all my clothes were as permanently wet as those of a seaman in the days of sail. There must be a special virtue in sweat, cooling one spiritually as well as physically.

Quive-Smith might stay for weeks. I couldn't bear the thought of returning to the burrow. I determined to take to open country again. I am not persuading myself of that. I really meant to go on the run, desperate though my chances were. Considering my appearance, to live and move at all would have been a hundred times harder than my original escape. Then I was believed to be dead and nobody was looking for me; now the police would be on me at the first rumour of my presence. But I wasn't going back. I intended to stalk around the downs, hiding in barns and in gorse, and living, if there were no other food, upon the raw meat of sheep. I could keep Quive-Smith under observation until such time as he returned to London or wherever else his undoubted ability to increase the rottenness in a rotten world should be required.

I watched the living-room until the child went to bed. Then the major joined Patachon in front of the fire, and Patachon's wife entered with two huge china mugs of cider. All three settled down to newspapers. There was nothing more to be learned.

I sidled towards the gable end, the weight of my body taken on shoulder and thigh, left hand on the coping and right hand testing the slates ahead lest one should be loose. I was concerned, God help me, with the noise of a single slate sliding down the roof into the gutter! A few feet from the end there was a subsidence beneath me. The slates sagged. I seemed to be floating on a heavy liquid that moulded itself to me, suddenly became brittle and crashed to the floor of the barn. For an instant I swung from the coping and then that too gave way. Five feet of stone tile, a solid expanse of slate, and myself roared down on to a pile of iron drinking troughs. It sounded like the collapse of a foundry.

I found later that I had reopened the wound in my shoulder and suffered various cuts and bruises, but at the time I was only shaken. I picked myself up from that welter of ironwork and dashed to the open door of the barn. I didn't go through it. Quive-Smith had thrown up the window of the living-room, and his long legs were already over the sill. My only thought was that he mustn't know I was still in this part of the country. The dogs started barking and jumping against their chains. Patachon opened the front door and stumped over the threshold, flashlight in hand.

I retreated into the barn and dived under the drinking troughs. They were ranged side by side, so that there was room for me between any two, and covered by the slates and rubble from the roof. Quive-Smith and the farmer entered the barn immediately afterwards.

'Damn 'un!' stormed Patachon, observing the damage, ''tis that beggarin' murderer after my cheeses. Over t' barn and down to dairy! I knew 'e was a stealin' of 'em. Over t' barn and down to dairy!'

I don't suppose he had lost an ounce, but farmers always suspect something is being stolen from them; there are so many things to steal. Quive-Smith obligingly agreed with me.

'Oh, I don't think there was anybody on the roof,' he said. 'Look at that!'

I knew what he was pointing at – a broken beam. It hadn't even broken with a crack. It had just given way like a sponge of wood dust.

'Death-watch beetle,' said the major. 'I met the same thing in the East Riding, by Jove! Tithe barn it was. Poor chap broke his bloody neck!'

It didn't ring quite true, but it was a gallant attempt at the right manner.

'Rotted!' agreed Patachon in a disgusted tone. 'Damn 'un, 'e's rotted!'

'Got to happen some time,' answered Quive-Smith. 'We ought to be thankful no one was hurt.'

'Bin there three 'underd years,' grumbled Patachon, 'and 'e 'as to come beggarin' down on *our* 'eads!'

'Oh, well,' the major said cheerfully. 'I'll turn to in the morning and give you a hand. Nothing to be done now! Nothing at all!'

I heard them leave the barn, straining my ears to analyse their two individual treads, making absolutely certain that one of them did not remain behind, or return. I heard the front door of the farm shut and bolted, and waited till the silence of the night was restored, till the faint noises of windows opening and bedroom doors closing had ceased, till the rats began to scutter over the floor of the barn. Then I crawled to the door and out, creeping like a nocturnal caterpillar along the angle between the wall and the filthy courtyard.

For what I then did I have no excuse. I had begun to think as an animal; I was afraid but a little proud of it. Instinct, saving instinct, had preserved me time and again. I accepted its power complacently, never warning myself that instinct might be deadly wrong. If it were not the hunted could always escape the hunter, and the carnivores would be extinct as the great saurians.

Gone was my disgust with my burrow; gone my determination to take to open country whatever the difficulties of food and shelter. I didn't think, didn't reason. I was no longer the man who had challenged and nearly beaten all the cunning and loyalty of a first-class power. Living as a beast, I had become as a beast, unable to question emotional stress, unable to distinguish danger in general from a particular source of danger. I could startle a dog fox, move as quietly and sleep as lightly, but the price I paid was to be deprived of ordinary human cunning.

I had had a bad fright. I was hurt and shaken. So I went without thinking to Safety – not to the form of safety adapted to the case, but to Safety in general. And that meant my burrow; darkness, rest, freedom from pursuit. I hadn't a thought – any more than, I suppose, the fox has such a thought – that the earth might mean death. Under the influence of panic when Quive-Smith shot me I had behaved in the same way, but then it was excusable. I didn't know what the devil I was up against, and to seek general Safety was as sound as any other move. To seek it now was simply a reflex action.

I took, of course, the most beautiful and cunning route; the animal could be trusted to perform that futility to perfection. I went through water and through sheep. I waited in cover to be sure there was no pursuit. I knew finally and definitely that there was no pursuit; that I was alone on the down above my lane. Then I covered the last lap with extreme caution and entered my burrow with attention to every dead leaf and every blade of grass.

All the next day I remained underground, congratulating myself on my good fortune. The stench and dirt were revolting, but I endured them with a holy masochism. I persuaded myself that in three or four days I could open my door and cleanse and dry the den, and Asmodeus would come back and we could live peacefully until it was safe for me to hang around the ports and get out of the country. My hands were all right again, showing little deformity. The left eye was still queer, but the right was so foul, filmy, and bloodshot that the difference between them was no longer remarkable. A shave and haircut were all I needed, and then I could pass anywhere as a criminal who had just celebrated his release from prison with a two-day binge.

After nightfall I heard some activity in the lane, and sat with my ear to the ventilator. I couldn't translate the noises. There were two men, but they did not speak to each other. I expect they whispered, but owing to the curve of the little tunnel I could not hear so slight a sound. Something heavy was being moved, and once I heard a thud against the door. My thoughts played with the idea of a man-trap, a log perhaps that would fall on my head; they were certainly building something in the runway I had once used. Since I used it no longer I felt very clever and secure. I told myself that I was disappointed, merely disappointed, for they would wait another week or two for the result of their trap and I should have to stay underground.

All the time, as I now see, I was conscious of extreme terror and my heart was beating as if I had been running for my life. Only by an effort did I stop myself talking aloud. I am very clever, I was saying to myself over and over again. They'll find themselves run in for murder, I said, if they catch somebody else. And then the terror came up in my throat, for there was silence in the lane and little bits of earth were falling down my bolt hole into the inner chamber.

I lay between the two dens, watching the trickle of earth and listening to the quick strokes of a chopper. A man, as I thought, jumped or fell into the hole, and a wave of rubble rolled down to the bottom. I reached for my knife, and waited. He's at my mercy, I said, I can make what terms I like. I was obsessed with the idea of talking, not killing. A reasonable man, I told myself. He'll see sense. He plays chess.

There was no further sound, none at all. The man had stuck in the hole or died. I crept up the slope of foul earth and lay on my back, poking an ash-pole up the chimney as far as the twist. It didn't meet the body I expected; it met a hard obstruction. I withdrew myself as far as I could, for fear of some trap or explosive, and poked harder. The thing felt solid with a smooth under surface. I lit a candle and examined it. It was the sawn end of a tree trunk which had been jammed into my hole.

I crawled to the door and pushed against it; nothing moved. Then I felt a sense of panic with which was mingled relief that the end had come at last. I intended to rush out and let them shoot. A quick death, merited. I took the axe that had hollowed out the sandstone and drove it between the planks of the door. It turned. I ripped off the planks. On the far side of them was an iron plate. It rang hollow except in the centre. They had jammed it in place with a baulk of timber, the other end of which rested against the opposite bank of the lane.

I don't know what happened to me then. When I heard Quive-Smith's voice I was lying on the bag with my head on my arms, pretending to myself that I was thinking things out. I was controlled, but my ears were drumming and my skin oozing cold sweat. I suppose that if one sits on hysteria long enough and hard enough, one loses consciousness. Something has to give way, and if the mind won't, the body must.

Quive-Smith was saying:

'Can you hear me?'

I pulled myself together and sloshed a handful of water over my head. There was no point in keeping silence; he must have heard me battering on the iron. The only thing to do was to answer him and play for time.

'Yes,' I said, 'I can hear you.'

'Are you badly wounded?'

Damn him for asking that question then! I should have found it very useful later if I could have persuaded them that I was suffering from a neglected wound and incapable. As it was, I answered the truth:

'Nothing much. You hit a whisky flask with a leather jacket behind it.'

He muttered something that I could not hear. He was speaking with his mouth close to the ventilation hole. If he jerked his head, the voice was lost.

I asked him how he had found me. He explained that he

had gone straight from the barn to the lane on the off chance that I had been responsible for the broken roof and that he might see me returning to my mysterious hiding-place.

'Simple,' he said, 'so simple that I was very much afraid that it was what you meant me to do.'

I told him that I had never attempted to kill him, that I could have done it a dozen times if I had wished.

'I suppose so,' he replied. 'But I counted on you leaving me alone. You would only have exchanged me for the police, and it was obviously wiser to persuade me that you had gone. You did, as a matter of fact.'

His voice had a weary harshness. He must have been in fear of his life all the time that he was at the farm. A braver man and a cleverer than I am, but without – I was going to write ethics. But God knows what right I have to claim any! I have neither cruelty nor ambition, I think; but that is the only difference between Quive-Smith and myself.

'Couldn't you give me a cleaner death than this?' I asked.

'My dear fellow, I don't want you to die at all,' he said, 'not now. I am so glad you had the sense not to break out while I was sealing you up. This position has taken me by surprise as well as you. I can't promise you anything, but your death seems wholly unnecessary.'

'The only alternative is the zoo,' I answered.

He laughed at this for a nervous, uncontrollable moment. Lord, he must have been relieved to know where I was!

'Nothing so drastic,' he said. 'I'm afraid you wouldn't survive in captivity. No, if they take my advice, I shall be ordered to return you to your position and friends.'

'On what condition?'

'Trifling – but we needn't go into that yet. Now, how are you off for food?'

'Reasonably well, thank you.'

'No little delicacies I can bring you from the farm?'

I nearly lost my temper at this. The man's voice had just the right touch of concern; there was but the tiniest shade of irony to tell me that he was thoroughly enjoying his own acting. He would have brought me anything I asked, I have no doubt. For the cat-and-mouse act to be subtle enough to please his taste, it had to be hardly distinguishable from genuine kindness.

'I think not,' I answered.

'All right. But there's no need for you to suffer any more.'

'Look here!' I said. 'You won't get any more out of me than your police did, and you can't stay here indefinitely. So why not get it over?'

'I can stay here for months,' he answered quietly. 'Months, you understand. I and my friend are going to study the habits and diet of the badger. The large piece of timber which is holding your door is for us to sit on. The bush placed in front of your door is a hide for the camera, and there will shortly be a camera in it. I'm afraid all these preparations are wasted since nobody ever comes into the lane. But if anyone should – well, all he will see is my friend or myself engaged in the harmless study of the life of the badger. We might even get a nice young man with a microphone and have him tell the children what Bertie the Brock keeps under his tail.'

I called him a damned fool, and told him that the whole countryside would be consumed with curiosity – that all their doings would be public property in twenty-four hours.

'I doubt it,' he answered. 'Nobody at the farm pays any attention to my innocent rambles. Sometimes I go out with a gun, sometimes not. Sometimes on foot, sometimes in the car. Why should they guess I am always in this lane? They have never seen you. They won't see me. As for my assistant, he has no connexion with me at all. He is staying in Chideock and his landlady thinks he is a night watchman at Bridport. He isn't as careful in making his way here as I should like. But we can't expect a paid agent to have our experience, can we, my dear fellow?'

This 'dear fellow' of his infuriated me. I am ashamed to remember that I rammed my axe against the door in anger.

'How about that?' I asked.

'It makes surprisingly little noise,' he said coolly.

It did, even in my closed space. He explained that there were felt and plywood over the iron.

'And if you think it out,' he added, 'what would happen if anyone did hear you? That disagreeable peasant who owns the field over your head, for example? You would compel me to remove the pair of you, and to arrange the bodies to show murder and suicide.'

It was true enough – so true, at any rate, that there was little object in pointing out that he couldn't get at me without running a grave risk himself. He held the only fire-arm and all the cards. He could foresee a more or less satisfactory outcome if he killed me; but if I killed him I could foresee nothing but murder on my conscience, and death or disgrace eventually at the hands of the service to which he belonged. Psychologically I was at his mercy. My mind cowered.

'We must stop talking now,' he said. 'No conversation in daylight will be our rule. I shall be on duty from 10 a.m. to 8 p.m., and we shall talk during the last couple of hours. My assistant will be on duty the rest of the time. Now, let me make the position perfectly clear. I cannot, I expect, prevent you forcing your way out over the top of the door. But if you do, you'll be shot before you can shoot, and closed up again in your cosy home. Your back-door is very thoroughly blocked, and if we hear you working we shall cut off your air. So be careful, my dear fellow, and don't lose heart! Quite calm – that's the watchword. Your release is certain.'

I sat for hours with my ear to the ventilator. I didn't expect to learn anything, but hearing was the only one of my senses which could keep in touch with my captors. So long as I heard them, I had the illusion that I was not wholly defenceless, that I was planning, gathering data for an escape.

I heard the twittering of birds at dawn. I heard a crackle as Quive-Smith adjusted or trimmed the screen of dead thorn outside my door. Then I heard a low mutter of voices which I translated as the sound of Quive-Smith's colleague taking over the watch from him. They couldn't, of course, keep to their schedule on that first day. The major had presumably to telegraph a report.

The new man sat quite still. I imagined his figure as a silhouette thrown against the darkness of the door. I had only seen him at a distance. I thought of him as dark and thick, as a contrast to Quive-Smith, who was fair and tall. I was quite wrong.

All the time that I crouched at the ventilator, my mind had been drifting over the wildest images of escape, enveloping them, rejecting them, concentrating finally upon the two practical schemes. The first, as Quive-Smith had suggested, was to cut a passage diagonally upwards over the top of the door. I took one of my long spits and drove it through the red earth. So far as I could tell, it passed over the top of their plate; but the knowledge was useless. As he had said, if I stuck out my head I would be shot – and, by the tone of his voice, I knew he did not mean killed, but deliberately crippled. The final break-through was bound to be so noisy that the watcher would have ample warning.

The second and far more likely way of escape was by the bolt-hole. They hadn't caged me so neatly as they thought.

Their tree-trunk had not blocked the whole length of my tunnel; only its vertical section between the surface and the twist. The passage quarried through the sandstone was open. All I had to do was to cut a new passage through the earth, and surely I could work at that so silently that not a sound would be heard outside.

I crawled into the choked inner chamber and began to dig with my knife. There was no room to use the axe; I was kneeling on the pile of muck and earth with my body filling the whole tunnel. Very silently and carefully, catching earth and stones in my hand, spending minutes in wearing through some root that I could have cleared with a jerk, I went at the job of digging a tunnel parallel to the tree trunk. The roar of my breath, thumping and gasping like the Diesel engines that had carried me to England, was by far the loudest sound.

The air was foul, for the draught between ventilator and bolt-hole no longer existed. The carbon dioxide that I breathed out collected between my shoulders and the working surface. My energy steadily diminished. I cleared a foot of clay and broken sandstone, and then had to return to the ventilator to breathe. On the next shift I cleared six inches; on the next three; on the next, again three. But there I interfered with the laws of geometrical progression, and faded out before I reached the ventilator.

I had insisted to myself that my sensation of extreme lassitude was sheer slackness; but now it was quite obvious that my body would collapse, try what I might in the way of compulsion, if I didn't allow it to obey the laws that governed its intake of oxygen. God knows what I was breathing in that muck-heap! If I had the exact figures of work and rest, no doubt some chemist would be able to work it out. Since I had only moved out of the burrow for a few hours in thirteen days, there must have been many gases besides carbon dioxide.

I came to after an unknown lapse of time. In the original den there was plenty of air so long as I did not work at anything too long or too fast. The ventilator was a passage some four feet long and curving down from the bank to the side of the den. It had a diameter large enough for Asmodeus to go in and out, but so small that I was always amazed he could.

It seemed to me at the time that I kept a remarkable control over myself. I concentrated on breathing in and out by the ventilator, forcing my mind to remain blank, to stay in that state where all activity is inhibited by shock and it is freed to wander through space obsessed by trivialities. I felt that I was, to use a horrid phrase, captain of my soul. I had hardly been tested. The only periods, I suspect, when a man feels captain of his soul are those when he has not the slightest need of such an organ.

For short intervals, separated by lengthy halts to breathe, I worked at the old chimney. There was no space to swing or thrust, nowhere to put the earth that fell. It was like trying to burrow through a sandhill, impossible to breathe, impossible to remove the debris. I could have obtained more air by boring another hole through to the lane (though it wouldn't have done me much good in the inner chamber), but I dared not give them a direct view into the burrow. The one strength of my position was that they could never see what I was doing.

The day passed quickly. Time drags only when one is thinking fast, and all my mental processes were slowed down. I was lying by the ventilator when night fell and Quive-Smith wished me a cheerful good evening.

'Everything has gone splendidly,' he said. 'Splendidly!

We'll have you out of there in an hour. Free to go home, free to live on that lovely estate of yours, free to do anything you like. I'm very glad, my dear fellow, I have a great respect for you, you know.'

I replied that I doubted his respect, that I knew him to be a good party man.

'I am,' he agreed. 'But I can admire such an individualist as you. What I respect in you is that you have no need of any law but your own. You're prepared to rule, or to be suppressed, but you won't obey. You are able to deal with your own conscience.'

'I am not. But I see what you mean,' I said.

'You must be! A man in your position to commit what you described in the subsequent proceedings as a sporting stalk! And then calmly pitching a spy on the live rail at Aldwych!'

I kept silence. I didn't know where this was leading. I hated the philosophy he was ascribing to me; it was a travesty of the truth.

'I'm not blaming you in the least for defending yourself,' he went on. 'The man was worthless, and got in your way. What other result could there have been? I should be disappointed – really, I mean it – to find a lot of sloppy scruples in such an anarchial aristocrat as you.'

'That's your morality rather than mine,' I answered.

'My dear fellow!' he protested. 'There's all the difference in the world! It's the mass that we are out to discipline and educate. If an individual interferes, certainly we crush him; but for the sake of the mass – of the State, shall I say? You, you don't give a damn for the State. You obey your own taste and your own laws.'

'That's true enough,' I admitted. 'But I have respect for the rights of other individuals.'

'Of course. But none at all for the nation. Admit it now,

my dear fellow, you could get along perfectly well without any State!'

'Yes, damn you!' I answered angrily – I hated his pseudo-Socratic cross-examination. 'Without the shameless politicians who run this country or the incompetent idiots who would like to, or your blasted spotlight Caesars.'

'There's no point in being rude,' he laughed. 'Limelight has just the same effect on the emotional public as Westminster Abbey and a sovereign's escort – and it's a lot cheaper. But I'm glad you have grown out of these rather childish allegiances, because we shan't have any difficulty in coming to terms.'

I asked him what his terms were. He pushed a paper down the ventilator with a stick. I collected it, also with a stick.

'Just sign that, and you are free,' he said. 'There is only one serious restriction. You must undertake not to leave England. We leave you at complete liberty in your own country. But if you attempt to reach the Continent, this will begin all over again and we shall show no mercy. I think you'll admit that, after what you did, it's a reasonable condition.'

I asked him for a light. I wasn't going to use up candles and oxygen. He poked his torch down the hole without hesitation. He knew by this time that he could force me to give it back.

The form they wished me to sign was lengthy but simple. It was a confession that on the -th August I had attempted to assassinate the great man, that I had undertaken this with the knowledge (they didn't quite dare to write approval) of the British Government, and that I had been released without any punishment on condition that I remained in England. The document was signed by their chief of police, by witnesses, and by a London notary public attesting my signature, although it did not then exist. He was, to judge by his address, quite a reputable notary too.

It was a good torch, and I employed it for the next quarter of an hour in getting order into my excavations. Then I gave it him back together with his paper. There was no object in showing indignation.

'I wouldn't try to persuade you,' he said, 'if you had the usual bourgeois nationalism. A man of your type would rather be a martyr. But since you don't believe in anything but yourself, why not sign?'

I told him that I cared for public opinion.

'Public opinion? Well, we shouldn't publish this document unless there was imminent danger of war and your government was acting its usual morality play. And from what I know of the English public's temper in time of crisis, they would probably make you a popular hero.'

'They possibly would,' I answered. 'But I don't sign lies.'

'Now, now, no heroics!' he begged me, in his blasted patronizing manner. 'You're a good Englishman, and you know very well that truth is always relative. Sincerity is what matters.'

I blame myself for being drawn into argument with him, but what else could I do? I was glad to hear a cultured voice, even his, after so much solitary confinement. It was, in a sense, not unlike being stuck in the club with some bore whose opinions are very left or very right. You can't do anything but listen to the man. You know he is wrong, but since you argue from the standpoint of individuals and he argues about a mythical mass, there is no common ground. And it's utterly impossible to explain yourself.

I lay no stress on the great physical weariness and discomfort to which I was subject. They gave him an enormous advantage over me in intellectual power, but he had that in any case. He drove me gently from one untenable position to another. He might have been a kindly doctor investigating a moral delinquent.

'I think,' he said at last, 'that it would make it a lot easier for both of us if you told me why you attempted assassination.'

'I told your people long ago,' I retorted impatiently. 'I wanted to see whether it was possible, and his death would be no great loss to the world.'

'You did then intend to shoot,' he said, accepting my statement quite naturally. 'I couldn't really help you, you see, till you had admitted that.'

I perceived that I had given myself away to him and to myself. Of course I had intended to shoot.

Their methods of interrogation are devastating to the muddle-minded – ninety per cent of us, whatever class we belong to. It's easy to make a man confess the lies he tells to himself; it's far harder to make him confess the truth. And when by their technique the truth has been dragged from him, he is so plastic and demoralized that he will accept any interpretation the questioner chooses to put upon it. The process is equally immoral and effective whether used by psycho-analysts or secret police. They make us see our own motives, and in the horror of that exposure we are ready to confess to any enormity.

I had been through all this before, of course, but at the hands of much coarser and less intelligent examiners than Quive-Smith. Physical torture merely increased my obstinacy. I was so occupied in proving to myself that my spirit was superior to my body that the problem of whether my intelligence had not been hopelessly over-shadowed by my emotions did not arise.

'Yes,' I admitted. 'I intended to shoot.'

'But why?' he asked. 'Surely political assassination settles nothing?'

'It has settled a good deal in history,' I said.

'I see. A matter of high policy then?'

'If you wish.'

'Then you must have talked it over with someone?'

'No. I went alone, on my own responsibility.'

'For the sake of your country?'

'Mine and others.'

'Then even though your government knew nothing about you, you were acting in a sense on their behalf?'

'I don't admit that,' I said, seeing where he was heading.

'My dear fellow!' he sighed. 'Now, you say you don't sign lies. Let me make your mind a little clearer, and you will see that I don't want you to. You have a number of friends in the Foreign Office, haven't you?'

'Yes.'

'You sometimes give them an informal report on your return from trips abroad. I don't mean that you are an agent. But if you had any interesting impressions you would pass them to the right man over the lunch-table?'

'I have done so,' I admitted.

'Then suppose you had succeeded and we had hushed the assassination up, would you have informed your friends that he was dead?'

'Yes, I expect so.'

'You do, you see, consider yourself a servant of the State,' he said.

'Not in this matter.'

'Oh dear, oh dear!' complained Quive-Smith patiently. 'A man with your experience of foreign society shouldn't have this English dislike of reasonable conversation. It is precisely and only in a matter of such importance that you consider yourself a servant of the State. In your daily routine you do not. You are an individualist obeying his own laws. Yet you admit that in this matter you acted for reasons of State and that you intended to inform the State.'

I repeat that I could not escape from him, that I was imprisoned in a space eight feet by four feet high by three feet wide. The fact that he was free and I was buried alive gave me a sense of inferiority to him. Of course it did. Obviously it did. Yet why should it have? I knew that he understood nothing which mattered to me, that he had not the faintest idea of my scale of values. Therefore, myself being sure of those values, our physical circumstances should have made no difference.

I see now that he was destroying a great deal of nonsense in my mind. It was possibly that, more than anything else, which gave me the sense of wriggling at the end of a hook.

'But I did not act at the orders of the State,' I said.

'I haven't asked you to sign your name to that. With the knowledge of the government, is the phrase. That wouldn't be a lie at all. We needn't even stick to those words. With the knowledge of my friends – how would that be?'

'It isn't true.'

'I'm not suggesting you were paid. No, I think you undertook this, as you say, more or less in a sporting spirit!'

'I told you so,' I said.

'Ah, yes. But a sporting assassination! Now, really, you wouldn't believe it yourself, you know.'

'Why not?' I asked furiously.

'Because it is incredible. I want to know why you hate us to such a degree that you were ready to murder the head of the State. What were your motives?'

'Political.'

'But you have admitted that you care nothing for politics,

and I believe you implicitly. Perhaps we mean the same thing. Shall we say that your motives were patriotic?'

'They were not,' I answered.

'My dear fellow!' he protested. 'But they were certainly not personal!'

Not personal! But what else could they be? He had made me see myself. No man would do what I did unless he were cold-drawn by grief and rage, consecrated by his own anger to do justice where no other hand could reach.

I left the ventilator, and lay down with my head at the entrance to the inner chamber; it was the most privacy I could attain. His voice murmured on, grew angry. I didn't care. I was fighting against the self-knowledge he had forced upon me. At last he was silent, and I surrendered to misery.

I will try to write of this calmly. I think that now I can. I am a man who has loved once, and did not know it till she was dead. Perhaps that is not quite correct. I loved with all my heart, but had little self-consciousness about it – not, at any rate, compared to the ecstasy and glory which love meant to her. I was too disciplined, too civilized. I loved her as a Chinese mandarin might love a flower, beautiful in itself, unquestionably beautiful to live with.

When I heard of her death, I did not weep. I told myself immediately that love was an illusion. I grieved that so exquisite a work of nature had been destroyed. I grieved, in my conscious mind, with that same sorrow which I would have felt had my house, in which fifteen generations have lived, been burned – an irreparable, terrible sense of loss, transcending any injury, but no hot, human grief.

That, I say, is what I thought I felt. He who has learned not to intrude his emotions upon his fellows has also learned not to intrude them upon himself.

Yet I was mad with grief and hatred. I describe myself as

then mad because I did not know it. The tepidity of my sorrow was not indifference; it was the blankness which descends upon me when I dare not know what I am thinking. I know that I was consumed by anger. I remember the venomous thoughts, yet at the time I was utterly unaware of them. I suppressed them as fast as they came up into my conscious mind. I would have nothing to do with them, nothing to do with grief or hatred or revenge.

When I went to Poland I considered that I was taking quite a conventional course: to go out and kill something in rough country in order to forget my troubles. I had not admitted what I meant to kill. I did not admit it till Quive-Smith destroyed all possible self-deception.

She was so swift and sensitive. She could do no other than make a generous cause her own. Impulsive, spiritual, intelligent, all at such energy that she seemed to glow. A boy who saw such things told me that sometimes there was a visible halo of light around her. To that I am insensible. But, as I remember her, life extended beyond her body; neither touch nor sight could quite surely say – here she begins and here she ends. Her skin was not a surface; it was an indefinite glory of the palest rose and orange that chose to mould itself to those tense limbs.

She knew, I suppose, that in our mixture of impulse and intelligence we were alike. Her emotions governed her brain; though she would support her side with devastating logic, logic had nothing to do with her devotion. I should never have suspected that of myself, yet it is true. I have never taken sides, never leaped wholeheartedly into one scale or the other; nor do I realize disappointments, provided they are severe, until the occasion is long past. Yet I am ruled by my emotions, though I murder them at birth.

They caught her and shot her. Shot her. Reasons of State.

Yes, I know, but surely the preservation of such an individual is why we suffer, why we fight, why we endure this life. Causes? Politics? Religion? But the object of them is to produce such a woman – or man, if you will. To put her, her, against a wall – there is no cause that justifies an act so satanic. It is the life of such a creature which justifies any cause she chooses to adopt. What other standard have we? In all history has any man become a Christian because he was convinced by the Athanasian creed? But how many millions have been convinced by the life of a single saint!

I declared war upon the men who could commit such sacrilege, and above all upon the man who has given them their creed. How ridiculous that one person should declare war upon a nation! That was another reason why I hid from myself what I was doing. My war was a futile cause to me, to be smiled at sympathetically just as I used to smile at her enthusiasms. Yet in fact my war is anything but futile. Its cost in lives and human suffering is low. Seek out and destroy the main body of the enemy – and I should have destroyed it but for a change of wind.

I realized that since the day I was caught I had been defeated only by the loneliness and uncertainty. How could I admit to myself that I, the mandarin, was declaring war, that I, the unfeeling lover, had been so moved by the death of my beloved? That I, the civilized, scrupulous sportsman, was behaving like an ice-cream merchant with a knife?

Well, all that, as I lay in the silence of my temporary grave, was at last admitted. And so I passed to a spiritual offensive.

The offensive! Again, how ridiculous for a man who hadn't the room to stand up to feel on the offensive! But I was no longer the passive sufferer. My demoralization had been appalling while I knew no cause for which I suffered.

Now that I did know – my God, I remembered that there were men at Ypres in 1915 whose dugouts were smaller and damper than mine!

I do not know how long I lay there. I passed in thought over great distances of geographical space, over all the movement of my attack and retreat, but there was no activity in myself or the outer world by which time could be measured. At last I was roused by the perceptible rising of the water.

I thought at first that there must be heavy rain outside, and thrust a stick down my two drains to clear them. It met hard obstructions. Of course they had found and plugged the holes. That added to my discomfort – if anything could – but put me in no danger. The water would leak out under the door as soon as it rose to the height of the sill.

I spoke through the ventilator almost with gaiety. I was buoyed up by a feeling of light-heartedness, much the same, I suppose, as that of a penitent after confession. I knew why I was in my burrow. I felt that what I had done had been worthwhile.

'Anyone there?' I asked.

Quive-Smith answered me. The night had passed, and the other man had come and gone.

'You will merely succeed in giving me pneumonia, my dear fellow,' I said.

'Delirium,' he replied, 'won't change your hand-writing.'

It was the first time that I had annoyed him; he let me hear the cruelty in his voice.

I started to burrow again, hoping with my new courage to get to the surface sometime after nightfall. But it was not courage that needed multiplying; it was oxygen. I had to leave the work at shorter and shorter intervals, and to allow a greater margin of safety than before. If I fainted with my head in the sea of mud on which my sleeping-bag was floating, it would be all over.

When I could do no more, I rolled up the useless bag and spread a layer of tins on top of the bundle. On them I sat, crouched forward with the nape of my neck against the roof and my elbows on my knees. It was uncomfortable, but the only alternative was to lie full-length in the water. That would have made me no wetter than I was, but a lot colder. I shivered continuously. Nevertheless the temperature in the den must have been well above that of the outside air. The poets are wrong when they describe the grave as cold.

In the evening, the third since my imprisonment, Quive-Smith tried to make me talk, but I would not. At last I heard his colleague take over from him. The major wished me good-night, and regretted that I should force him to increase my discomfort. I didn't understand what he meant. After that there was silence – a silence more complete than any I had experienced. Even at night and buried, my ears caught faint noises of birds and beast.

The night dragged on and on. I began to suffer from hallucinations. I remember wondering how she had got in, and begging her to be careful. I was afraid that when she left, they might think she was I, and shoot. Even while I was off my head I could not conceive that anyone would hurt her for being herself.

They passed, those dreams. It was the growing effort of breathing which drove them away. I was desperate for air. I couldn't make the man hear me when I spoke, so I hammered lightly on the door. A shaft of light showed at the angle of the ventilator. Quive-Smith had blocked it before he left.

'Stop that!' ordered a low voice.

'I thought it was still night,' I answered idiotically.

I meant that I wouldn't have hammered on the door if I had known it was already morning. I didn't want some innocent person involved in the reckoning.

'I have orders to break in and shoot if you make a noise,' he said stolidly.

He had the flat voice of a policeman in the witness-box. From that, and from the major's description of him, I was pretty sure of his type. He wasn't in this service from ambition and love of the game itself, both of which undoubtedly counted with Quive-Smith; he was a paid hand.

I told him that I was a wealthy man and that if I escaped I could make him independent for life.

'Stop that!' he answered again.

I thought of pushing a fat bank-note up the ventilator, but it was too dangerous to let him know I had money; he would have been in a position to force unlimited sums from me, and give nothing in return.

'All right,' I said. 'I won't talk any more. But I want you to know that when they let me out I won't forget any little favours you can show me.'

He made no answer, but he didn't put back the obstruction.

I hunched my rolled bag towards the ventilator, and sat down with my face pressed to it. The sun was shining outside. I could not see it, but in the curve of that imitation rabbit-hole the deep orange crystals of the sandstone were glowing with light. There was an illusion of warmth and space. The twenty-four inches of sand, being so close to and directly under my eyes, lost perspective. The minute irregularities became sandhills, and the tunnel a desert with the sun still bathing the horizon and the dark clouds of the Khamsin gathering overhead.

My watch had stopped, but I think it must have been

nearly midday before Quive-Smith came on duty. The first I heard of him was a shot – so close that I was sure he had potted something in the lane – and then the laughter of both men.

When dusk fell, he began to examine me for the fourth time. His approach was cordial and ingenious. He gave me a précis of the news in the morning paper, then talked of football, and so came round to his boyhood; he had, he said, been educated in England.

His personal reminiscences were frank, though he implied a lot more than he said. His mother had been an English governess. She felt socially inferior and morally superior to his father – a horrid combination – and had tried to make her son a good little Briton by waving the Union Jack and driving in patriotism with the back of a hairbrush – with the natural result that his affection for his mother's country never rose higher than the point of contact. He gave away nothing about his father; I gathered that he was some obscure baron. When, later, I came to know Quive-Smith's real name I remembered that his restless family had a habit of marrying odd foreign women, and had consequently been cold-shouldered by their peers. He had a Syrian for his grandmother. That accounted for the almost feminine delicacy of his bone structure.

He led me on to talk of my own boyhood, but as soon as I felt myself affected by the confidential atmosphere that he was creating I dried up. I knew his methods by now. There was never a chance that he could make me sign that paper of his, but he could – and it shows amazing technique – still make me wonder whether I wasn't being absurdly quixotic in refusing.

He threatened to block the ventilator again if I did not talk to him. I retorted that if he stuffed up that hole I should die; and, in case that should encourage him, I added that asphyxiation appeared to be a pleasanter death than any I could give myself.

I had not, in fact, the least thought of committing suicide now that I knew the object of my existence. Even during the first lost and hopeless days suicide had only been a possibility to which I gave as much consideration as to each of a dozen other plans. One does not, I think, kill oneself without a definite desire to do so. It is hardly ever an act to which a man must key himself up; it is a temptation which he must struggle against. I have more than my fair share of mental diseases, but the black suicidal depression doesn't happen to be one of them.

He laughed and said he would give me all the air I wanted, all the air I wanted through the sort of filter that was fit for me. He dropped his English manner completely. It cheered me enormously to know that I was getting on his nerves.

I heard him push some bulky object into the hole and ram it well down towards the curve. I didn't much care. I knew from experience that there was enough air stored in the burrow and leaking under the door to keep me going for many hours.

I remained quiet, considering whether or not to pull the obstruction down into the burrow. I could get at it. The tunnel was the shape of my arm bent at the elbow, and half as long again. But the risk was serious. If he caught and fixed my left arm as it groped upwards, he would not thereafter be so dainty in his methods of cross-examination.

I poked with a stick, and found the thing to be soft and stiff. I advanced my fingers inch by inch until they brushed against it and I snatched back my hand. I had touched, as I thought, an arrangement of wires and teeth, but before my arm was fairly out of the tunnel I realized what it really was.

The simultaneous mixture of terror and relief and anger made me violently sick.

Taking Asmodeus' head in my hand, I drew his remains into the den. Poor old boy, he had been shot at close quarters full in the chest. It was my fault. People who sat quietly in the lane were, in his only experience, friendly and had bully beef. He had been shot as he confidently sat up to watch them.

I was choking with sorrow and rage. Yes, I know – or one side of me knows – that it was the idiotic, indefensible love of an Anglo-Saxon for his animal. But Asmodeus' affection had been of so much harder price than that of a creature which one has fed and brought up from birth. Our companionship had a stern quality, as of the deep love between two people who have met in middle age, each looking back to an utterly unshared and independent life.

Quive-Smith cackled with laughter and told me that, really, I had only myself to blame; that he hoped I wouldn't be too proud to talk to him on the following evening. He couldn't, of course, have known that Asmodeus was my cat, but he had quite correctly calculated that I should draw his obstruction into the den and that I could never push it back. By God, if he had known the atmosphere I lived in he would never have thought that a dead cat could make it any worse!

When the other man had come on duty, I set about disentangling my stiffened body. While moving my roll of bedding I felt that I could not have stood up even if there had been head-room. I knelt in the mud with my hands on the door sill and tried to straighten my legs. My impression had been right – I had set with my knees two feet from my chin.

I had no need of sleep, for I had passed some hours of every twenty-four half dozing, half unconscious. During the night I worked on my body, and when at last it consented to open up I supported myself on toes and hands and practised those exercises which, I believe, business men are ordered to perform before breakfast. I stopped shivering and ate a solid meal of oatmeal moistened with whisky. I wished that I had thought of limited exercise before, but I had been demoralized by the filth of my condition. And there was no object for physical strength.

It seems ridiculous to say that by shooting Asmodeus Quive-Smith condemned himself to death; it was in a sense so slight a crime. Patachon would have shot the old poacher without hesitation. I should have grieved for him no less, but admitted Patachon's right. In the same way I admitted Quive-Smith's right to shoot me by the stream. I can neither defend nor explain the effect that the shooting of this cat had upon me. It released me. I had intended to escape by the chimney without bloodshed. From then on all my plans were directed towards a swift and deadly break-through into the lane. I was at last able to admit that all my schemes for escaping without violence were impossible. The only practical method was to kill the man on duty before, not after, I started digging.

The ventilator was my only means of physical contact with them. I meditated a number of ingenious decoys to persuade the major to thrust his arm down the hole. This idea of a trap had not, apparently, occurred to him, and it might work. But it would do me no good, I decided, even if I caught Quive-Smith. You can't kill a man quickly with only his arm to work on. He could yell for help.

To kill him through the ventilator? Well, there was only one way, and that was to straighten the curve so that I could shoot a missile up the tunnel. It was useless to poke at him with some improvised spear; to give instantaneous death I had to deliver a heavy weapon at a high initial velocity.

An iron spit at once suggested itself as the weapon. It would fly true for the short range of some three and a half feet between the point and his head; but it could not be fired from my catapult or from any rearrangement of its rubber. I had to have something in the nature of a bow.

None of my bits of wood served. There was no room to handle an ash-pole of such length that its bending would have the necessary force. A bow proper, or any method of propulsion by the resiliency of wood, was excluded. Bent steel or twisted rope might have done, but I had neither.

I looked over my full and empty tins in the hope of finding another source of power. Some were on my rolled sleeping-bag; some under Asmodeus. I had laid his carcase on a platform of tins. A last tribute of sentimentality. He could never have endured the mud. When I laid my hand on him I realized that in his body was power. He could take his own revenge.

I skinned Asmodeus and cut his hide into strips. I have always been interested in the mechanics of obsolete weapons, and guilty of boring my friends by maintaining the supremacy of the Roman artillery over any other up to the Napoleonic Wars. The engine that I now contrived was an extremely crude model of a hand-drawn ballista. I remember considering something of the sort for use on rabbits, but, since I felt more sympathy for them alive than dead, I never constructed it.

I made a square frame of which the uprights were two bricks and the horizontal bars two stout billets of ash fitting into roughly scraped grooves at the tops and bottoms of the bricks. Parallel to the bricks and on the inner side of them I twisted two columns of raw hide. Through the centre of each column was driven a long peg which projected three or four inches beyond the brick. A wide thong was attached to the tips of the two pegs as a bowstring joins the ends of a bow. The twisting and shrinkage of the strips of hide held the whole frame rigid and forced the pegs hard back against the bricks.

On the farther side of the bricks and lashed to them by square lashings was a strip of wood from a packing-case, in the centre of which I cut a semi-circular aperture. The method of firing the ballista was to lie on my back with my feet on the outer edges of this wooden strip. The point of the spit passed through, and was supported by the aperture; the ring of the spit was gripped in the centre of the thong by the thumb and forefinger of the right hand. Thus, by the pull between hand and feet the pegs were drawn towards my chest against the torsion of the columns of hide. When the spit was discharged, the pegs thudded back on the bricks, which were padded with cloth at the point of contact.

By the time I had made the machine it was morning, or later, and Quive-Smith was on duty again. I dared not practice for fear of noise, so I slept as best I could and waited for the evening examination. I intended to be polite, for I wanted information about the major's assistant. I hadn't the faintest idea what to do with him – I was in no position to take prisoners – but I had a feeling that he might be more useful to me alive than dead.

At the hour when Pat, Patachon, and their labourers had all retired to their respective firesides, Quive-Smith opened the conversation. After we had exchanged a few guarded commonplaces, he said:

'You're unreasonable, really unreasonable. I'm surprised at a man of your sense enduring such conditions!'

I noticed a touch of impatience in his voice. He had begun

to realize that watching badgers in a damp lane on November evenings was not an amusement that anyone would want to carry on for long. He must have wished that he had never thought of that invaluable confession.

'I can endure them,' I answered. 'You're the man who is suffering for nothing. I've come to the conclusion that if I sign that document of yours, you'll never have occasion to publish it. There isn't going to be any war. So it doesn't matter whether I sign or not.'

I thought that would appeal to him as a piece of British casuistry: to deny that I was uncomfortable, but to produce a hypocritical justification for getting more comfort. It was a text-book illustration good enough to take in the foreigner.

As a matter of fact no Englishman that I know would have signed his bloody paper – refusing partly from honour but chiefly from sheer obstinacy. He's a neurotic creature, the modern John Bull, when compared to the beef-and-ale yeoman of a hundred years ago; but he has lost none of great-grandfather's pig-headedness.

'You're perfectly right, my dear fellow,' said Quive-Smith. 'Your signature is a mere necessary formality. The thing will probably stay at the bottom of the archives till the end of time.'

'Yes, but look here!' I answered. 'I trust you not to talk. I don't know who you are, but you must be pretty high up in your service and have a sense of responsibility. But what about this other fellow? I may lay myself open to blackmail, or he may change sides.'

'He doesn't know who you are,' replied Quive-Smith.

'How can I be sure of that?'

'Oh, use your head, man!' he answered contemptuously – I was pleased that his voice no longer had its usual note of ironical but genuine respect. 'Is it likely? He doesn't even know who I am, let alone you. This morning he did his best to find out. I expect you tried to bribe him.'

'Is he English?' I asked.

'No, Swiss. A people, my dear fellow, of quite extra-ordinary stupidity and immorality. A very rare combination which only a long experience of democratic government could have produced. A Swiss agent is the perfect type of Shakespeare's Second Murderer.'

I refrained from the obvious gibe. Nobody could cast Quive-Smith as a First Murderer. He was definitely in the employing class.

I wanted to keep him talking, so that he wouldn't insist on my signing his document immediately. I asked him what was the matter with democracy.

He read me a long lecture, which degenerated into a philippic against the British Empire. I slipped in a provoca-tive word here and there to encourage him. He hated us like hell, considered us (he said it himself) as the Goths must have considered the Roman Empire, a corrupt bunch of moralizing luxury-lovers who could only hold their frontiers by exploiting – and that inefficiently – the enormous wealth and the suffering millions behind them. In fact it was a speech that would have gone equally well in the mouth of his boss's opposite number on the other side of Poland.

He even had the effrontery to invite me to join the winning side. He said that they needed in all countries natural leaders like myself; I had only to sign, and bygones would be bygones, and I should be given every chance to satisfy my will to power. I didn't tell him that natural leaders don't have any will to power. He wouldn't have understood what I meant.

I dare say he was sincere. I should have been a very useful tool, completely in their power. When you find an agitator who hasn't suffered poverty, it's sound to ask whether he has ever been in my position and what he has done that our police don't know and a foreign police do.

'I'll sign in the morning,' I said.

'Why not now?' he answered. 'Why suffer another night?' I asked him where on earth I could go. I told him that before I could be let loose on the public, he would have to bring me clothes, and, when I was decently dressed, take me to his farm to wash. All that couldn't be done at a moment's notice without arousing a lot of curiosity.

'I see your point,' he said. 'Yes, I'll bring you clothes in the morning.'

'And get that Swiss of yours away before we talk! That's what worries me most. I don't trust him a yard.'

'My dear fellow,' he protested, 'I wish you would give me credit for some discretion.'

When the Second Murderer had come on duty and settled down for the night, I started to practise with the ballista, stuffing a coat into my end of the ventilator so that the thud of the pegs could not be heard. The strips of hide had shrunk into even tighter coils. It was a more powerful weapon than I needed, and the devil to pull; I had to use both hands, my left on the shaft of the spit, my right gripping the ring, held horizontally so that it did not catch as it flew through the aperture. At a range of four feet the spit drilled clean through two tins of tomatoes and buried itself six inches in the earth. I shot it off less than a dozen times, for the construction was none too strong.

I unstopped the ventilator and fanned for an hour to change the air. Heaven knows whether it really made any difference, but it was worth trying since my next task was to persuade the Swiss to shut up his end of the ventilator, and keep it shut while I straightened the tunnel.

I began moaning and mumbling to shake his nerves a bit. When he ordered me to stop it, I said I would if he told me the time.

'Half-past two,' he answered sulkily.

I stayed quiet for another hour, and then went off my head again – sobs and maniac laughter and appeals to him to let me out. He endured my noises with annoying patience (hoping perhaps for that hypothetical reward) and compelled me to such a show of hysteria before he plugged the hole that I managed to get on my own nerves into the bargain. My acting was good enough to be a genuine release for my feelings.

The straightening of the tunnel was easy and quite silent. I dug with my knife and gathered the earth handful by handful. At intervals I let off some moans to discourage him from removing the plug. The curve vanished, and in its place was an empty hollow, like a rabbit's nest, with two mouths. His plug was a piece of sacking. I opened out its folds on my side without disturbing its position. I could breathe without difficulty and hear every sound in the lane.

I arranged my rolled sleeping-bag under my shoulder-blades, and lay on my back in the mud with the engine presented and the spit fitted to the throng. I had to be ready to fire the moment that a man's head appeared at the hole. The removal of the sacking would give me time to draw, and if anyone looked into the hole and noticed that its shape had been altered, that would be the last thing he ever noticed.

I hoped that the Swiss would leave the sacking alone. I felt no compunction in killing him, but if he removed the plug immediately before Quive-Smith's arrival I might not be able to cut my way out in time to surprise the major. I kept up enough muttering to prove that I was a nuisance and alive, but not so much that he would be tempted to pull out the sacking and curse me.

The light of morning gleamed through the folds. I waited. I waited, it seemed to me, till long after midday before Quive-Smith arrived. As a matter of fact, he was early – if, that is, he usually came at ten a.m.

For the first time I could hear all their conversation. At that hour in the morning they spoke in low voices and as little as possible.

'He has gone mad, sir,' reported the Swiss stolidly.

'Oh, I don't expect so,' answered Quive-Smith. 'He's just avoiding the crisis. He'll soon be calm.'

'Usual time tonight, sir?'

'If not, I will let you know. Your woman has been warned that you may be leaving?'

'Yes, sir.'

I heard his heavy steps sploshing off through the mud. All this time I was lying on my back and staring at the hole.

I cannot remember the slightest effort in drawing the ballista. There was a flash of light as he withdrew the plug. I started, and that slight jerk of my muscles seemed to pull the thong. Immediately afterwards his head appeared. I noticed the surprise in his eyes, but by that time I think he was dead. The spit took him square above the nose. He looked, when he vanished, as if someone had screwed a ring into his forehead.

I hacked at my end of the ventilator until it was large enough to receive my body, then crawled inside and burst through into the lane with a drive of head and shoulders. Quive-Smith was lying on his back watching me. I had my thumbs on his wind-pipe before I realized what had happened. The foot of spit that projected behind his skull was holding up his head in a most life-like manner. He hadn't brought any spare clothes. Perhaps he didn't intend me to live after he had my signature; perhaps he didn't believe that I would sign. The latter is the more charitable thought. He had a loaded revolver in his pocket, but that is no proof one way or the other.

I burned that scandalous document, then stretched myself and peered through the hedge over the once familiar fields. Pat was nowhere in sight, and his cows were grazing peacefully. Patachon was talking to his shepherd on the down. It was a damp November day, windless, sunless, of so soft a neutrality that, coming to it straight from disinterment, I couldn't tell whether the temperature was ten or thirty degrees above freezing-point. By Quive-Smith's watch it was only eleven. I ate his lunch. Behold, Sisera lay dead and the nail was in his temples.

I destroyed his screen of bushes and his camera (thorough though I knew him to be, I was surprised that he had really set the scene for his badger watching) and folded up the heavy motor-rug which kept him warm. Then I shifted the log that was jammed between both banks of the lane, and opened the door of the burrow. The stench was appalling. I had been out only half an hour, but that was enough for me to notice, as if it had been created by another person, the atmosphere in which I had been living.

Boiling some muddy water on the Primus, I sponged my body – a gesture rather than a wash. It was heaven to feel dry and warm when I had changed into his clothes. He had heavy whipcord riding-breeches, a short fur-lined shooting coat – Central European rather than English, but the ideal garment for his job – over his tweeds and a fleece-lined trench-coat over the lot.

When I was dressed I went through his papers. He had the party and identity documents of his own nation, with his real name on them. He also had a British passport. It was not in the name of Quive-Smith. He had put on that name and character for this particular job. His occupation was given as Company Director, almost as non-committal as Author. Anybody can qualify for either description, as every police-court magistrate knows; but they look impressive.

In a belt round his waist I found £200 in gold and a second passport. It had twice been extended by obscure consulates, but had neither stamps nor visas on it, showing that it had never yet been used for travel. That this passport was his own private affair was a fair assumption. The photograph showed his face and hair darkened with stain, and without a moustache. If I were in Quive-Smith's game, I should take care to have a similar passport; should he have a difference of opinion with his employers, he could disappear completely and find a home in a very pleasant little Latin country.

I held up any definite plans until after I should have interviewed the Swiss, but when I cut my hair and shaved I left myself a moustache exactly like the major's and brushed my hair, as his, straight back from the forehead. The name and identity of the Company Director might suit me very well.

I removed what was left of Asmodeus and buried him in the lane where he had lived and hunted, with a tin of beef to carry him through till he learned the movements of game over his new ground. I plugged the ragged hole made by my escape with my old clothes, my bedding and earth, and took from the den my money and the exercise book that contained the two first parts of this journal. Then I replaced the original door, and laid the iron plate against the bank of the lane, covering it with earth and debris. When the nettles and bracken grow up in the spring – and thick they will grow on that turned earth – there will be no trace of any of us.

I propped up Quive-Smith's body against a bush, where it was out of the way. Not a pretty act, but his siege had destroyed my sensibility. I had room for no feeling but immense relief. After dusk I walked round Pat's pasture to accustom my legs to exercise. I was very weak, and probably a bit light-headed. It didn't matter. Since all that remained was to take crazy risks, to be a little crazy was no disadvantage.

The tracks in the mud told me that the Swiss always entered and left by the top of the lane. There was no mistaking the prints left by Quive-Smith's abnormally small feet. I had been compelled to keep my own shoes, and the heels of his stockings were lumps under my soles.

I squatted against the bank in the darkest section of the lane and waited. I heard the fellow a quarter of a mile away. He was moving reasonably quietly where the lanes were dry, but had no patience with mud.

When he was a few paces from me I flashed Quive-Smith's torch on his face and ordered him to put his hands up. I have never seen such a badly frightened man. From his point of view he had been held up in the middle of nowhere by a maniac with a considerable grudge against him.

I made him keep his face to the hedge while I removed his documents, his pistol, and his trouser-buttons. I had read of that trick, but never seen it done. It's effective. A man with his trousers round his ankles is not only hindered; his morale is destroyed.

He carried a passport on him. I suppose those chaps always do. A glance at the first page showed me that his name was Muller, that he was naturalized English and that he was a hotel porter. He was a big man, fair-haired, with a fair moustache waxed to points. He looked as if he had modelled himself upon some ex-NCO of the Corps of Commission-aires.

'Is he dead?' the man stammered.

I told him to turn round and look, keeping him covered while I flashed the light on Quive-Smith's naked body. Then I put him back with his face to the hedge. He was shaking with fear and cold. His legs pulsated. He exhibited all the other involuntary reactions of panic. I had thrown his imagination out of control.

He kept on saying: 'What . . . what . . . what . . .'

He meant, I think, to ask what I was going to do to him.

'Who am I?' I asked.

'I don't know.'

'Think again, Muller!'

I placed the cold flat of my knife against his naked thighs. God knows what he thought it was, or what he imagined I meant to do! He collapsed on the ground, whimpering. I wanted him to keep his clothes reasonably clean, so I picked him up by one ear, and propped him against the hawthorn alongside Quive-Smith.

'Who am I?' I asked again.

'The Aldwych . . . the . . . the police wanted you.'

'Who is the man whose clothes I am wearing?'

'Number 43. I never met him before this job. I know him as Major Quive-Smith.'

'Why didn't Major Quive-Smith hand me over to the police?'

'He said you were one of his agents and you knew too much.'

That sounded a true piece of Quive-Smith ingenuity; it explained to a simple intelligence why it was necessary to put me out of the way, and why they were working independently of the police; it also ensured the Second Murderer's zealous co-operation.

'What were you going to do with my body that night?'

'I don't know,' he sobbed, 'I swear I don't know. I had orders to stay in the car every night until I heard a shot and then to join him.'

'Where did you get the iron plate?'

'I had it cut at Bridport on the morning when he first discovered you were here. I used to meet him outside the farm for orders.'

'How many years have you worked in hotels?'

'Ten years. Two as night porter.'

'Any dependants?'

'A wife and two tiny tots, sir,' he said piteously.

I suspected he was lying; there was a whine in his voice. And I felt that, considering the varied human material at their disposal, his employers wouldn't have chosen a family man for a job of indefinite duration.

'Where does your wife think you are?' I asked.

'Relieving at – at Torquay.'

'Does she believe that?'

'Yes.'

'She doesn't mind getting no letters from you?'

'No.'

'Doesn't it ever occur to her that you might be with another woman?'

'No.'

'Careful, Muller!' I said.

I merely raised the revolver to the level of his eyes. He shrieked that he had been lying. He pawed the air with his right hand as if he could catch the bullet in its flight. The wretched fellow feared death as he would a ghost. I admit that death is a horrid visitor, but surely distinguished? Even a man going to the gallows feels that he should receive the guest with some attempt at dignity.

'From whom do you take your orders?' I asked.

'The hotel manager.'

'No one else?'

'Nobody else, I swear!'

'What hotel?'

He gave me the name of the hotel and its manager. I won't repeat it here. It ought to be above suspicion, but for that reason, if no other, I have little doubt that our people suspect it. If they don't, they have only to check which of them in the last week of October lost a night porter who never returned.

'What crime did you commit?' I asked.

It was obvious that they had some hold on him in order to make of him so obedient and unquestioning a tool. Night porters, in my experience, are remarkable for their brusque independence.

'Assault,' he muttered, evidently ashamed of himself.

'How?'

'She invited me to her room – at least I thought she did. I shouldn't have done it. I know that. But I was going off duty. And then – then I went for her a bit rough-like. I thought she'd been leading me on, you see. And she screamed and the manager and her father came in. She looked a child. I thought I'd taken leave of my senses. She had just been laughing at me friendly, sir, when she came in of an evening, and I'd thought . . . I could have sworn that . . .'

'I know what you thought,' I said. 'Why didn't they charge you?'

'For the sake of the hotel, sir. The manager hushed it up.'

'And they didn't sack you?'

'No. The manager made me sign a confession and they all witnessed it.'

'So you have done what you were told ever since?'

'Yes.'

'Why didn't you get another job?'

'They wouldn't give me any references, sir, and I don't blame them.'

He was genuinely ashamed. He had come out of the realms of a panic-stricken imagination as soon as he was reminded of the real trouble of his everyday life. They had a double grip on the poor devil. They had not only ensured his obedience, but shattered his self-respect.

'Don't you see that they framed you?' I asked.

I was sure of it. Any really competent little bitch of seventeen could have managed those enigmatic smiles and performed that disconcerting change from temptress to horrified child.

'I'd like to believe it, sir,' he said, shaking his head.

No wonder Quive-Smith was exasperated by him!

I myself became a human being again. Muller might, for all I knew, have been a gangster of the most savage, and therefore cowardly type. I had to break him down. It wasn't only acting; I should have killed him without hesitation if he hadn't proved useful. But I was almost as relieved as he when I could lay brutality aside. I told him to pull up his pants, and gave him a bit of string to hold them and a cigarette. I kept the revolver in sight, of course, just to remind him that all in the garden was not yet roses.

'They know you at the farm?' I asked.

'Yes. I drove the major over there.'

'In what capacity? His servant?'

'Yes. He told them I was taking my own holiday on the coast.'

'Have you been at the farm since?'

'Once. I had lunch there the day that . . . that . . .'

'That you buried me alive.'

'Oh, sir! If only I had known!' he cried. 'I thought you were one of them – honest, I did! I didn't care if they murdered each other. It was a case of the more the merrier, if you see what I mean.'

'You seem to be pretty sure now that I'm not one of them,' I said.

'I know you're not. A gentleman like you wouldn't be against his own country.'

Wouldn't he? I don't know. I distrust patriotism; the reasonable man can find little in these days that is worth dying for. But dying against – there's enough iniquity in Europe to carry the most urbane or decadent into battle.

However, I saw what use Muller had been to his employers. A night porter must be able to sum up his customers on mighty little evidence, especially when they arrive without any baggage. He must, for example, know the difference between a duke and stock-pusher though they speak with the same accent and the latter be much better dressed than the former.

I explained to him that he might consider himself out of danger so long as his nerve did not fail; he was going down to the farm to tell Patachon that Quive-Smith had been called back to London, to pack his things, and to take them away in the car.

Quive-Smith had almost certainly warned his hosts that he might be off any day, so the plan was not outrageously daring. Muller had the right air of authority; with the rug over his arm, he looked trained and respectable in spite of being somewhat muddy. He was dressed in such a way that he could pass for a night watchman in Chideock or a man-servant on a holiday: a stout tweed suit, an old pullover of suede, and a stiff white collar.

The chief risk was that Muller, when he found himself in the farm, would decide that his late employers were more to be feared than I. That point I put to him with the utmost frankness. I told him that if he wasn't out of the house in a quarter of an hour I should come and fetch him and claim to be the major's brother. I also told him that he was useful to me just so long as nobody knew the major was dead, and that the moment when his usefulness ceased, whether in ten minutes or two weeks, would be his last.

'But if you are loyal to me for the next few days,' I added, 'you can forget that matter of criminal assault. I'll give you money to go abroad and never see your late employers again. They'll leave you in peace. You're no further use to them, and you don't know enough to be worth following. So there you are! Give me away, and I'll kill you! Play straight with me, and there's a new life open to you wherever you want to lead it!'

There were a good many holes in the argument, but he was in no state for analytical thinking. He was deeply impressed and became maudlin with relief. Quive-Smith was quite right about him; he was the perfect Second Murderer. He attached himself with dog-like simplicity and asked only to be allowed to obey.

He took the major's head while I took his heels, and we moved cautiously down into the road that ran along the foot of the hill. There, thankfully and immediately, we dropped our white burden in the ditch. I saw the sweat burst out on the back of Muller's thick neck as soon as he was convinced that we had not been seen.

At the five-bar gate where Patachon's private track swung across the home paddock to the farm we stopped. I told Muller that I should wait for him there, and should enter the car when he got out to open the gate. I gave him Quive-Smith's keys and I gave him a story to tell. The major was dining with friends in Bridport. He had learned that he had to go abroad at once. His address for forwarding letters was Barclays Bank, Cairo. I knew from a letter in his pocket that he kept an account with a branch of Barclays – and Cairo is a complicated town through which to trace a man's passage.

'But what will I do if they don't believe me?' he asked.

'Of course they'll believe you,' I answered. 'Why the devil shouldn't they?'

I was none too sure of that, but his best chance of success was to show the utmost confidence.

I gave him a pound to tip the girl who had made the major's bed – if there were such a girl – and another which he was to hand to Mrs Patachon for her daughter's savings bank.

'You know the little daughter?' I asked.

'Yes – Marjorie.'

'Give Marjorie a message from Major Quive-Smith: that she must remember not to bring her queen out too soon.'

'I don't understand,' he said.

'All the better. Explain to her that you don't understand what it means. But she will, and she'll laugh. Tell her not to bring her queen out too soon.'

It was perfectly safe advice to give a beginner at chess, and it would establish Muller's bona fides.

I let him cross the paddock and go round the corner of the barns into the yard; then I followed to watch, so far as possible, over my fate. This time there was no need to take extreme pains to hide myself – the dogs had an excuse to bark. I squatted behind a tree whence I could see the front door.

Mrs Patachon received the caller with surprise but no hesitation. She shut the door and there was no movement for five minutes – which I spent wishing I had cut the telephone wires. Then an oil-lamp was lit in an upper room, and I saw Muller pass back and forth across the window. He came out with a suit-case in his hand, followed by Patachon with a gun-case. Marjorie with the rug, and Mrs Patachon with a packet of sandwiches. The whole party were chattering gaily – except Muller, who was far too glum – and sending messages to the major. They entered the stable to watch Muller load and start the car, and I ran back to the gate.

'Where to, sir?' asked Muller.

In spite of his grip on the wheel his elbows were quivering like the gills of a fish – partly from reaction and partly from fear that his usefulness had come to an end. I was sorry to appear again as a ruthless killer, but there was a risk that he might try to rush the gate.

I told him to drive to Liverpool and to go easy with the traffic laws. Southampton was too close, and London too full of eyes. We picked up Quive-Smith and put him in the back of the car, under a rug.

My plans were straightening out, I was sure that nobody would call at the farm until letters and telegrams had remained a week or more without reply; anxiety would have to be very strong before any of the major's subordinates or superiors – if he had any superiors – ventured to intrude upon his discreet movements. When they did, and visited the lane, they could take their choice of three theories: that I had got away with Quive-Smith and Muller hard on my heels; that I had bribed the pair of them to let me go; or that they had killed me and in some way aroused the curiosity of the police.

We stopped for petrol at Bristol and Shrewsbury. On the way I wired an assortment of ironmongery to Quive-Smith, and dropped him into the Severn. I have no regrets. Reluctantly, belatedly, but finally I have taken on the mentality of war; and I risk for myself a death as violent and unpleasant as any he could wish for me.

We reached Liverpool in time for an early breakfast. The town was in its vilest mood, and I was glad that the major had dressed himself for exposure to the elements. A north-east wind gathered the soot, dust, and paper from the empty streets, iced them and flung them into the Mersey. The sullen yellow water gave a more bitter impression of cold than the blue of the Arctic. I felt greater confidence in the wretched Muller. On such a morning it was inconceivable that anyone would betray a person who intended to have him out of England before nightfall.

Putting up at a hotel, we breakfasted in our room. While Muller dropped off to sleep in front of the fire, I spent a couple of hours practising the signature on Quive-Smith's passport. For convenience I still write of him and think of him as Quive-Smith, though there is possibly no one but myself, Saul, Muller, and a handful of people in a corner of Dorset who ever knew him by that name. The signature I practised and the identity I had taken were those of his normal British self – the nondescript company director.

This English name of his was signed in a spidery, flowing script which, with a fine nib, was not at all difficult to imitate. My forgery wouldn't have taken in a bank manager, but it was good enough for an embarkation form or a customs declaration – especially since it would be written on cheap paper with an office pen.

The passport photograph was not very like me, but near enough. No shipping clerk would question it. The common type of Quive-Smith and myself is manifestly respectable and responsible.

I woke up Muller and offered him a drink. He turned out to be a teetotaller – another advantage, I suppose, to his employers. I took him with me to the bathroom, and while I washed off the accumulated filth of weeks (keeping the revolver handy on the soap-dish) I made him sit on the lavatory seat and read me the shipping news.

We had ships sailing that afternoon for New York; for the West Indies; for Gibraltar and Mediterranean ports; for Madeira and South America; for Tangier and the East. All countries for which I needed a visa were excluded, and all voyages longer than a week. Gibraltar, Madeira, and Tangier remained – and Madeira was a dead-end, to be avoided if possible.

How to lose Muller was a difficult problem. I had promised him his life and freedom, but it was going to be a hard promise to keep. He had only one set of documents; he was too stupid to ship himself as a stowaway without being caught; he hadn't the sense or presence to bluff. Whatever port he entered and left would be sure to have full particulars of him. I didn't much care whether he were traced or not – I was sure that his employers would take no further interest in him after he had answered their questions – but I wanted to put off that questioning as long as possible.

I wondered what Quive-Smith would have done had he found himself saddled with Muller as the only witness to murder or bribery. The answer was not far to seek. He would have pushed Muller overboard on the night before reaching port, and concealed his absence. That seemed an admirable solution. It would convince them that I really was Quive-Smith – in case they doubted it – and would put an end to all search for the hotel porter.

This, then, was my plan; but instead of pushing him overboard wherever was convenient, I had to push him overboard within reach of land and with the means of landing. There were two places where that could be done –

the point near the mouth of the Tagus where the Cintra hills come down to the sea, and Cape St Vincent.

I sent for a barber to give me a decent haircut, and, as soon as we left the hotel, bought a monocle which disguised, or rather emphasized and accounted for the glassy stare of my left eye. Then I led Muller round the shipping offices – an eccentric holiday-maker and his secretary-valet. I asked as many silly questions as a Cook's tourist; I hoped, I said, to be able to wave to an old friend who lived in Portugal. The shipping clerks explained to me patiently that it depended where my friend lived, that Portugal had a long seaboard, and that in any case the largest of handkerchiefs could not be seen at a couple of miles. They were surprisingly polite; they must, after all, spend much more time instructing prospective customers in elementary geography than in selling them tickets.

I found out what I wanted to know. The Gibraltar ship wouldn't do; it passed the Tagus in the morning, and Cape St Vincent shortly after sunset. The Tangier ship, a slow old tub with one class only, was more suitable. It passed the Tagus between 9 p.m. and midnight.

I had a look at the plans. The steering gear was aft on the main deck, and between its housing and the stern was the usual small and private space where lovers park their chairs, provided they can endure the exaggerated motion of the ship. There would be no room for lovers on this trip. The company director and his companion were going to spread themselves and their deck-chairs over that space, and be rude to anyone who disturbed their privacy.

We booked two adjoining state-rooms with a bath between, and then did our shopping. I provided Muller and myself with bags and necessaries for the voyage. I bought a collapsible rubber boat with a bicycle pump to inflate it, a pair of strong paddles in two pieces and a hundred feet of light rope, all packed in a large suit-case. Muller, naturally, thought the boat was for my own escape; I didn't disillusion him. Then I put the car into storage for a year, and we went on board.

Down St George's Channel and across the Bay I had no need to trouble myself about Muller's whereabouts. He had never made an ocean voyage. The ship was a mere 8,000 tons. The sea was very rough. I occupied the vile heaving rail at the stern, just to establish a squatter's rights over it, and after a painful morning acquired my sea-legs. It was a blessing to have none of my usual biliousness. I was free to spend my time eating, drinking, and washing; I needed as much of the three pleasures as the ship provided.

On the third night out from Liverpool we passed Finistierra, and awoke to a pale blue world with a rapidly falling swell; the grey-green hills of Portugal lay along the eastern horizon. I routed my secretary-valet out of bed, and fed him breakfast. Then we occupied the two deck-chairs at the stern. I spread out my rugs and legs as awkwardly as possible, and through my monocle stared offensively at anyone who dared to pick his way over them. None of the passengers showed the slightest desire to join us.

In the late afternoon I gave Muller a couple of lemonades to brace his courage, and asked him what he wanted to do. Would he rather return to London and report himself, or vanish off the face of the earth? He was very nervous at the thought of not going back to tell what he knew of Quive-Smith's death.

'You'll have to explain why you told so many lies at the farm,' I reminded him. 'The family can bear witness to the fact that you were alone. Nothing prevented you from telephoning to London.'

He promptly begged me to take him with me wherever I was going. The man was quite incapable of standing by himself. As soon as he was detached from one support, he began waving frantic tentacles in the hope of gripping another.

I replied that I couldn't take him; he would have to disappear by his own individual route.

'They would follow me,' he cried. 'I would never have any peace, sir.'

'They won't follow you if they think you are dead,' I said.

I explained to him the plan: that he and the rubber boat were to be thrown overboard when we were a couple of miles from shore, and that I would give him £500 with which to start a new life. He brightened up a bit at the thought of money, but then was appalled by the difficulties facing him when he reached the shore.

Well, there was one thing Muller could be trusted to do: to follow orders. So I gave them.

'Your clothes will be in the boat,' I said. 'When you land, put them on. Rip the boat to bits, and hide them under a rock. Walk to Cascaes and take the electric train to Lisbon. Don't go to a hotel. Spend the night where you do not have to register. If you drink a coffee at any of the bars in the centre of the town, I expect some way of passing a discreet and pleasant night will occur to you. In the morning go to the docks to meet an imaginary friend who is arriving by ship. Pass back again through the customs as if you came off the boat and get your passport stamped. Then buy yourself a visa and a ticket for any country you want to visit, and leave at once by another ship.'

'But suppose they look for me in Lisbon,' he said. 'They will see that I entered and left.'

I explained to him that I should make it clear he was dead;

once they were sure he had never landed in Tangier, they wouldn't look for him in Lisbon or anywhere else.

He seemed to think that he was a person of importance, and that they would ransack the world to find him. I repeated that so long as they thought Quive-Smith alive, they would not spend an hour or a fiver hunting for a useless agent whom they believed to be dead.

'I know too much,' he protested.

'You don't know a damn thing,' I answered. 'I doubt if you even know what country you were working for.'

'I do, sir,' he said, and mentioned it.

By God, it was the wrong one! I suppose it's a commonplace that the underlings of a secret service should not even know the nationality of their employers, but it seemed to me remarkably clever.

I told him he was wrong, and proved it by the major's papers. After that I had no more trouble except his natural funk of the sea.

We were a little ahead of schedule, and the Cintra hills were in sight at sunset. That suited me well enough; we could get the job over while the passengers were at dinner. So that no one should be sent in search of us, I told the chief steward that I wasn't feeling well, and that my secretary would be looking after me.

Muller undressed in the cabin, and I tied the money round his neck in a fold of oilskin. As soon as the alleyways were clear we took the suit-case on deck, and unpacked and inflated the boat in the shelter of the deck-house. We could see lights on shore, so he knew in which direction to row. I made Muller repeat his orders. He had them pat, and he put them crudely. Then I lashed his clothes and the paddles to the bottom of the boat, and looped the other end of the long line around his waist.

The wash of a ship isn't inviting. The poor devil sat on the rail shivering with cold and panic. I didn't give him time to think, but hurled the boat over and snapped at him that he would drown if he let the line tauten. I saw the boat, a dark patch bobbing on the white wash, and I saw him come to the surface. A second later, the only sign that he had ever existed was a dressing-gown lying on the deck. Good luck to him! With the right job and a positive boss, his qualities of Second Murderer should ensure for him a secure and happy life.

I returned to my state-room with the suit-case and dressing-gown, and went to bed – his bed till midnight and my own till morning. When the cabin steward called us, he naturally assumed that my secretary was already up and about.

The day was abominably long. There was some doubt whether we should arrive at Tangier in time for passengers to land that night; if we didn't, I had no hope of keeping Muller's disappearance secret. I missed breakfast and passed the morning in concealment, acting on the general principle that nobody would think of us if neither were seen, but that, if one were seen, there might be enquiries about the other. At lunch-time I entered the saloon to tip my table steward, but refused to eat. I told him that both I and my secretary had been badly upset by our food, and that I had prescribed for us a short period of starvation. There was nothing like starvation, I boomed pompously, for putting the stomach right; that had always been our experience in India.

While the cabin steward was off duty between two and four, I packed the bags and took them on deck. Cape Spartel was in sight. The purser confirmed that we should certainly be able to leave the ship before the customs closed. I collected the two landing-cards. Then again I went into hiding until we dropped anchor.

As soon as the tender arrived and the baggage had been carried off the ship, I visited and tipped the cabin steward in a great hurry. He was not exactly suspicious, but he felt it his duty to ask a question.

'Is Mr Muller all right, sir?'

'Good heavens, yes!' I answered. 'He packed up for me and took everything on deck. He's on the tender now with the baggage.'

'I hadn't seen him all day, sir,' he explained, 'so I thought I had better ask.'

'I haven't seen much of him myself,' I replied testily. 'I understand he found an old friend in the engineers' department.'

He let it go at that. Muller was my servant. I was eminently respectable. If I saw nothing wrong, nothing could be wrong.

The worst danger was on me now. Lest the tally should be wrong, I had to surrender two landing-cards while appearing to surrender only one. I am no conjurer; the simplest card trick defeats me if it demands sleight of hand. This confounded business worried me far more than the job of throwing Muller overboard. I loitered near the head of the gangway, hoping there would be a rush of passengers descending to the tender. There never was. Most had already left the ship. The rest came one by one.

I dashed into the smoking-room and stuck the two landing-cards lightly together with the gum from a penny stamp; they were of thin cardboard, and I hoped that the Assistant Purser who was collecting them wouldn't notice that I had shoved two into his hand. If he did notice, I proposed to say that Muller was already on the tender and that he must have gone down the gangway without surrendering his card. If someone then had a look at the tender and found he wasn't there, I could only show amazement and pray that I didn't find myself in the dock on a capital charge.

I went through the entire murder trial while I stuck these two cards together: the black and incontrovertible evidence that I had concealed Muller's absence, the discovery of my identity, and so on. My fantasy had developed as far as shooting my way out of the magistrate's court when I walked down the gangway and the Assistant Purser received my two cards without a glance. Ten minutes later I was on the Tangier mole, surrounded by a yelling mob of coffee-coloured porters draped in burnouses of sacking.

Passing through customs, I had my entry carefully noted. I took pains to see that the French immigration official wrote down the company director's name correctly spelled. From then on there could be no shadow of doubt that Major Quive-Smith had duly entered Tangier, and alone.

As for Muller, his late employers' discreet enquiries at the offices of the line would be duly passed on to the ship. The stewards would remember that Muller had not been seen for twenty-four hours. The Assistant Purser would remember that when he checked the landing-cards he found two suspiciously stuck together. The engineers' department – if the steward remembered my remark – would say they had never heard of Muller. And it would be reported back to Liverpool that there was indeed grave reason to fear that something had happened to Mr Muller. Whoever had put the enquiry on foot, having found out what he wanted to know, would then laugh at the serious faces of the directors, and explain that Mr Muller was perfectly safe and sound, and that – well, any yarn would do! Mr Muller, for example, had feared to be cited as co-respondent and had taken steps to conceal his movements.

I drove to a hotel, deposited my baggage, and booked a

room for a week, telling the proprietor that I had a little friend in Tangier, and that, if I didn't turn up for two or three nights, he was not to be surprised. I had an enormous meal at his excellent restaurant. Then I put a razor, a bottle of hair-dye and another of stain into my pocket, and walked off into the deserted hills. Besides money, the only thing I carried out of my past life was this confession, for I began to see in what manner it might be useful.

I do not think that in all my life I have known such relief and certainty as in a valley between those sun-dried hills, where the water trickled down the irrigation channels from one hand-dug, well-loved terrace to another, and no light showed but the blazing stars. My escape was over; my purpose decided, my conscience limpid. I was at war – and no one is so aware of the tranquillity of nature as a soldier resting between one action and the next.

I buried that company director's passport and my own, with which I have probably finished for ever. I shaved off my moustache, stained my face and body, and dyed my hair. Then I slept till dawn, my face in the short grass by the water's edge, my body drawing strength from that warm and ancient earth.

In the morning I strolled to the upper town, where I had not been the night before, and completed my change of identity. I bought a thoroughly Latin suit, spats, and some beastly pointed shoes, posting my other clothes in a parcel addressed to the Public Assistance Committee, Rangoon. I trust there is such a committee. I went to a barber, who duly doused me with eau-de-cologne and brushed my luscious black hair straight back from my forehead. When this was over, my resemblance to the photograph on Quive-Smith's Latin passport was a lot closer than my resemblance to the company director.

The regular packet was leaving that day for Marseilles. I got a French visa on my passport (my fatherland is as awkward as all other American countries – I can travel nowhere without a visa) and bought a ticket in my new name. Since I had no baggage, it was easy to bluff my way on to the ship without passing the control. Thus there was no record for inquisitive eyes that this courteous and scented gentleman had either entered or left Tangier, and no means of connecting him with Quive-Smith. I think they will be looking for their vanished agent between Atlas and the Niger.

My Dear Saul,

I write this from a pleasant inn where I am accustoming myself to a new avatar. I must not, of course, give you any clue to it; nor would the trail of the gentleman I describe as Latin — even assuming it could be followed — lead to where or what I am.

I want these papers published. If necessary, have them brushed up by some competent hack and marketed under his name. You won't, of course, mention mine, nor the name of the country to which I went from Poland and to which I am about to return. Let the public take its choice!

My reason for publishing is twofold. First, I have committed two murders, and the facts must be placed on record in case the police ever got hold of the wrong man. Second, if I am caught, there can never again be any possible question of the complicity of H.M. Government. Every statement of mine can, at need, be checked, amplified, and documented. The three parts of the journal (two written accidentally and the last deliberately) form an absolute answer to any accusation from any quarter that I have involved my own nation.

Forgive me for never telling you of my engagement nor of the happy weeks we lived in Dorset. I first met her in Spain a couple of years ago. We hadn't reached the point of an announcement in The Times, *and we didn't give a damn about it anyway.*

The ethics of revenge? The same as the ethics of war, old boy! Unless you are a conscientious objector, you cannot condemn me. Unsporting? Not at all. It is one of the two or three most difficult shots in the world.

I begin to see where I went wrong the first time. It was a mistake to make use of my skill over the sort of country I understood. One should always hunt an animal in its natural habitat; and the natural habitat of man is — in these days — a town. Chimney-pots should be the cover, and the method, snapshots at two hundred yards. My plans are far advanced. I shall not get away alive, but I shall not miss; and that is really all that matters to me any longer.

Must-read classic thrillers from
GEOFFREY HOUSEHOLD

Available now from Orion